Julian Symons is primarily remembered as a master of the art of crime writing. However, in his eighty-two years he produced an enormously varied body of work. Social and military history, biography and criticism were all subjects he touched upon with remarkable success, and he held a distinguished reputation in each field.

His novels were consistently highly individual and expertly crafted, raising him above other crime writers of his day. It is for this that he was awarded various prizes, and, in 1982, named as Grand Master of the Mystery Writers of America – an honour accorded to only three other English writers before him: Graham Greene, Eric Ambler and Daphne du Maurier. He succeeded Agatha Christie as the president of Britain's Detection Club, a position he held from 1976 to 1985, and in 1990 he was awarded the Cartier Diamond Dagger from the British Crime Writers for his lifetime's achievement in crime fiction.

Symons died in 1994.

BY THE SAME AUTHOR
ALL PUBLISHED BY HOUSE OF STRATUS

CRIME/SUSPENSE

THE 31ST OF FEBRUARY
THE BELTING INHERITANCE
BLAND BEGINNINGS
THE BROKEN PENNY
THE COLOUR OF MURDER
THE END OF SOLOMON GRUNDY
THE GIGANTIC SHADOW
THE IMMATERIAL MURDER CASE
A MAN CALLED JONES
THE MAN WHO KILLED HIMSELF
THE MAN WHO LOST HIS WIFE
THE MAN WHOSE DREAMS CAME TRUE
THE NARROWING CIRCLE
THE PAPER CHASE
THE PLAYERS AND THE GAME
THE PLOT AGAINST ROGER RIDER
THE PROGRESS OF A CRIME
A THREE-PIPE PROBLEM

HISTORY/CRITICISM

BULLER'S CAMPAIGN
THE TELL-TALE HEART: THE LIFE AND
    WORKS OF EDGAR ALLEN POE
ENGLAND'S PRIDE
THE GENERAL STRIKE
HORATIO BOTTOMLEY
THE THIRTIES
THOMAS CARLYLE

The **Killing** of **Francie Lake**

Julian Symons

HOUSE OF
STRATUS

For
GEORGE SIMS

INTRODUCTION

The French call a typewriter *une machine á ècrire*. It is a description that could well be applied to Julian Symons, except the writing he produced had nothing about it smelling of the mechanical. The greater part of his life was devoted to putting pen to paper. Appearing in 1938, his first book was a volume of poetry, *Confusions About X*. In 1996, after his death, there came his final crime novel, *A Sort of Virtue* (written even though he knew he was under sentence from an inoperable cancer) beautifully embodying the painful come-by lesson that it is possible to achieve at least a degree of good in life.

His crime fiction put him most noticeably into the public eye, but he wrote in many forms: biographies, a memorable piece of autobiography (*Notes from Another Country*), poetry, social history, literary criticism coupled with year-on-year reviewing and two volumes of military history, and one string thread runs through it all. Everywhere there is a hatred of hypocrisy, hatred even when it aroused the delighted fascination with which he chronicled the siren schemes of that notorious jingoist swindler, Horatio Bottomley, both in his biography of the man and fictionally in *The Paper Chase* and *The Killing of Francie Lake*.

That hatred, however, was not a spew but a well-spring. It lay behind what he wrote and gave it force, yet it was always tempered by a need to speak the truth. Whether he was writing about people as fiction or as fact, if he had a low opinion of them he simply told the truth as he saw it, no more and no less.

This adherence to truth fills his novels with images of the mask. Often it is the mask of hypocrisy. When, as in *Death's Darkest Face* or *Something Like a Love Affair*, he chose to use a plot of dazzling legerdemain, the masks of cunning are startlingly ripped away.

The masks he ripped off most effectively were perhaps those which people put on their true faces when sex was in the air or under the exterior. 'Lift the stone, and sex crawls out from under,' says a character in that relentless hunt for truth, *The Progress of a Crime*, a book that achieved the rare feat for a British author, winning Symons the US Edgar Allen Poe Award.

Julian was indeed something of a pioneer in the fifties and sixties bringing into the almost sexless world of the detective story the truths of sexual situations. 'To exclude realism of description and language from the crime novel' he writes in *Critical Occasions*, 'is almost to prevent its practitioners from attempting any serious work.' And then the need to unmask deep-hidden secrecies of every sort was almost as necessary at the end of his crime-writing life as it had been at the beginning. Not for nothing was his last book subtitled *A Political Thriller*.

H R F Keating
London, 2001

Chapter One

Boy Kirton spent the most important part of his life in a box nine feet long by seven wide by eight high. The floor of the box was covered by carpet of soft, delicate grey. There was a desk, not a big one, and this desk was placed cater-cornered so that it formed a triangle with the meeting of two walls. He sat within this triangle in a position which for some reason he felt to be better than if, for example, he had sat with the light coming over his left shoulder from the metal-framed window which looked down seven floors into a side street. The box contained one other chair, a hat and coat stand, and on the window wall an abstract painting by a friend of Kirton's who worked in the art department of an advertising agency. Sets of printers' galleys hung on the wall behind him. The box had one brick wall. The three others were partitions, made of wood up to a height of four feet, and above that a lattice-work of wood and frosted glass. In one of these partition walls a door was set, and this door led out into a larger box of identical shape. Here the floor covering was haircord, there were filing cabinets, desks, noiseless typewriters. Another metal window looked out into the same side street. In this larger box lived Kirton's assistant Jack Smedley, Smedley's assistant Charlie Owens, and two girls who were sometimes called secretaries and sometimes research workers. This box again had one brick and three partition walls, and it differed from Kirton's only in the fact that there was clear and not frosted glass in the wall separating the box from the corridor.

At five minutes to three Boy Kirton looked at his watch, got up and walked crab-wise round the desk out of his cater corner. He opened the door of his box, which said *Charles Kirton, Editor*, told one of the girls that he would be with Mr Gaye, opened the door of the larger box, which said *Crime Today, Editorial*, and turned left down the corridor, passing other partitions of wood and clear glass. He was a neat man of medium height, dark-haired, with small feet and hands. He wore a suit of plain dark grey, a white shirt, a blue tie. There were shadows under his eyes, but otherwise his smooth round face looked remarkably young. He made a right turn in the corridor and, at a point where the glass partitions gave way to the opacity of wood, opened a door and went in. This door had no name on it.

The carpet in the room he entered was of the same grey as that in Boy Kirton's box, but it was so thick that the feet sank into it. It was a long way across the grey carpet to the big desk, Ocky Gaye's desk, that stood commandingly almost in the middle of the room. Behind this desk there was a chair, behind the chair a great picture window extending almost the whole width of the room. Looking out of this window you could see Fleet Street, a couple of minutes' walk away. On the desk there stood the Epstein head of Ocky, bronze hair crisply curling, eye sockets sternly sunken, nose aquiline but boldly fleshy, large lips bent upwards at the edges in the hint of a smile. The John portrait hung on the wall that faced the desk, violent in reds and browns, its expression one of scowling concentration.

A man and a woman looked up as he came in. Francie Lake said, "He should be back any minute, Boy. Are you staying or going?"

"He said he wanted to see me at three o'clock. I may as well stay."

She nodded. "You were saying, Dex?"

"I'm worried about the paper. Circulation-wise it's keeping up but some of the things in it, well, I don't know what they do to our readers, but by God, they frighten me." In the voice of Dexter Welcome, editor of *The Plain Man,* there was nowadays always the hint of a whine. Through the piggy geniality of the features, the soft brown eyes that were somehow misted over so that they did not seem to see you clearly, the figure whose plumpness was reduced by a good suit, it was still possible to discern the lean, eager Dexter Welcome who had come over ten years earlier from a Fleet Street national to edit *The Plain Man* because it was a crusading paper that would allow him to say what he wanted. "I wondered if you could have a word with him, Francie."

It was a mistake, Boy Kirton thought, to say things like that to Francie Lake, who sat there now with one still extremely elegant leg crossed over the other, dark eyes sparking and snapping, long nose inquiring, sharp mind assessing, summarising, and generally rejecting everything that was being thought or said. In a sense Francie was, as you might say, one of the boys. She would drink with them in the *British Volunteer,* talk as one of themselves. Yet she was also a person apart, and that was not simply a matter of sex. Although Francie's involvement with Ocky had ended long ago, it was still unwise to say things to her that Dex might safely have said to Jimmy Crundle, or to Boy Kirton himself. In her hoarse, rusty voice she said now, "That's the sort of thing you have to do for yourself, Dex. But if circulation is up I'd have thought that was the answer."

Restless, half-listening to what was said yet wishing to convey that he had no part in it, he wandered over to the picture window and stood looking down and across. Opposite, a little to the left, and of course quite a long way below, a poster outside a bomb site that was being excavated said A PLAIN MAN SPEAKS TO YOU. From the middle of the poster, a little odd from this angle, Ocky Gaye looked out.

3

It depends on the angle, Boy Kirton thought, it all depends on the angle. Look at it from up here, and you've cut it down to size. Look at it from the street and you get an impression of something enormous, as compelling as that old Kitchener poster. And why talk about cutting it down to size, which is the right size anyway?

"Ten past three," Dex said. "I've got a paper to get out. Where are those galleys?"

His words were immediately answered. The door opened and Jimmy Crundle came in. "Galleys, Dex? Boy put them in my hands two minutes ago, most urgent, for Mr Welcome, and he's in with the chief, the chief wants to see them."

Dex accepted the galleys, spread them out on a table beneath the John portrait, said gloomily, "Come and look."

They came over and stood beside him, staring down at the three cover variants on the table. Each of them had a masthead that said *The Plain Man.* In Which Ocky Gaye Tells You the Truth. Ninepence Weekly. Below was written in a violent script, "Corruption in the Church." In the first proof the rest of the cover was taken up by a crude drawing of a leering clergyman holding a young boy by the arm, about to take him into the vestry. The second proof was photographic. It showed a girl, obviously a prostitute, talking to a clergyman in a Soho street, with a couple of other tarts looking on. The third cover was in the form of a strip cartoon. A clergyman was taking a confirmation class, and had dismissed all the pupils except one girl. "Will you stay behind, Mary, for further instruction," he asked. The last picture showed him with one hand on her knee, saying, "Now, you mustn't be frightened…"

"I like the cartoon," Francie Lake said.

"The choir boy or the cartoon," Jimmy Crundle agreed. Kirton, standing close, caught the essential Crundle smell, compounded of smoke and drink and food and sweat. He moved away a little. "Jam tarts are just jam tarts, don't mean much any more. How d'you get the picture?"

"Ray Pillin dressed up an out-of-work actor, paid him ten quid. What do you think, Boy?"

"So the photograph's a fake," Boy Kirton said. "What about the story?"

"The story, oh storywise it's terrific." The words gushed out of Dex's mouth as though forced through a gap in a dam. "Absolutely bags of stuff, letters every week about Revs getting their parishioners in the family way, the Bishop of Bumdom and his favourite choirboy, all that stuff. Storywise, it's right on the ball and the picture, well, we're just leaving readers to draw their own conclusions, after all. But still don't you think, I mean to say, don't you think these are all a bit much?"

Silence. Jimmy said unsympathetically, "You're the editor, Dex."

"Oh, yes, of course, and of course I know we want to sell the paper."

"And we're operating in a falling market," Francie said rustily. "So we start pulling our punches, does that make sense?"

"I think I like the cartoon." Jimmy Crundle was still poring over the covers. "I mean, I want to know what happens next."

Dex brightened. His self-questioning was as easily erased as the words on a tape recorder. "For that see text, particularly the Randy Rector of Revingham."

Boy Kirton took a complete set of proofs over to the window and began to look through them. It was very much *The Plain Man* as usual, Ocky's editorial, "The Cant and Hypocrisy of the Church," which had probably been written by Dex with Ocky putting the finishing touches, a Red spy article, another on a revolt of scientists in a nuclear research establishment against their inadequate pay, two pages of readers' letters, an article about sex in naturist communities ("Next Week: 'I was attacked in a Holiday Camp,' Sensational Revelations"), an attack on a trade union that had sent a worker to Coventry, a violent piece about tax dodgers, a short story, some cheese-cake, a double page spread for the article about corruption in the Church, which quoted from a number of letters whose writers appeared only under initials. Then more readers' letters and more cheese-cake at the end.

The Plain Man had been born at a time that seemed to Boy Kirton impossibly remote, a time when he was still at school writing triolets and villanelles, and totally unconcerned by the activities of a young middle-aged politician named Octavius Gaye, who had walked out of the House of Commons after a speech in which he attacked both Government ("these lacklustre nonentities grinning with self-satisfaction at their success in making the world unsafe for human beings to live in") and Opposition ("their passion for regimentation has been successfully applied to themselves, so that the majority of them have turned into wooden puppets – not surprising when you consider their original mental equipment – who say Aye or Nay unanimously at the jerking of a few unscrupulous string-pullers"), and also Parliament itself as "this fraud and fake, this sewer of ignorance where everybody talks and nobody listens, where every speaker represents one vested interest or another, and nobody speaks for the plain men and women of Britain." That had been Ocky Gaye's last speech as an Independent MP. He had called his constituents together, repeated his observations about Parliament, and told them that he meant to make a direct appeal to the people of Britain. Six weeks later, the first issue of *The Plain Man* appeared, the cornerstone, as you might fancifully put it, of the building in which they sat. Plain Man Enterprises now included two children's papers and a sporting weekly, an astrological magazine and a paper for farmers, as well as the crime weekly which Kirton edited.

Plain Man Enterprises was not an empire comparable in size to those of Fleetway or Odhams. In a sense it was not a magazine empire at all so much as the expression of a personality which, as his immensely successful television programme, "Ocky Gaye's Half Hour" testified, had meaning and value for millions of viewers. Just what sort of personality it was, Kirton had been wondering ever since he had first met Ocky Gaye at a cocktail party when he had come down from Oxford nearly eight years ago.

"You've had your fun, written your sonnets, cost somebody a small fortune. All right. Now what are you going to do with your life, boy?"

His answer had been consciously impertinent, but then it was an impertinent question. "Earn enough to write some more sonnets."

"But you've got to make a living, right? Come and work for me. You'll make enough to write sonnets."

"And if I don't like it?"

"If you don't like it there's no law that says you have to stay."

Had he liked it? He only knew that he had stayed, and that he had written no more sonnets. From that first meeting he had brought away an impression of squat bulk, of twinkling slate-blue eyes and overwhelming good humour. It was a week later, when they ate lunch together in a restaurant where Ocky ordered all the expensive dishes, that he was exposed to the full vulgarian charm.

"Plovers' eggs? Of course you want them, boy. Look how much they cost."

"But I don't like them much. Why should I eat them?"

"They cost more, so they're better. It's the only test. Take herrings now, they tasted wonderful the way my old Gran used to cook them, fried in oatmeal. Do you get them in a place like this? Of course you don't. Why not? Too cheap. You get trout instead, and you say how good they are. If herrings cost as much as trout they'd be a delicacy. So you order plovers' eggs to show your contempt for money. Besides, it's my money, so why not spend it?"

"I thought you were an apostle of the Plain Man."

"So I am. I want everybody to be able to eat plovers' eggs. Then I can go back to eating herrings fried in oatmeal. Is that logical?"

"No." They both burst out laughing.

During the whole of lunch he received Ocky's uninterrupted attention. People with well-known faces and even better-known names passed by the table, stopped, spoke, but Ocky Gaye dismissed them briefly and went on talking earnestly to his young guest. In the years that followed Boy Kirton was to see this gift exercised often, and in the most diverse circumstances, but it never failed to impress him. And impressive, too, were the sudden shifts from jokes to seriousness. Lunch was good humoured and humorous. Seriousness came with the coffee.

"Shall I tell you what's the matter with this country, boy? The people are still asleep. They were lulled to sleep after the war, when wages were high and jobs were easy, and they haven't woken up to what's going on all round them. In government you get jobs for the boys, the trade union boys with one lot, the old school tie boys with another. The big boys can fiddle out of taxation, the small ones can't, they get a slice forcibly removed from their pay packet every week. The whole world's a fiddle nowadays, everyone's on the crook. You're saying that isn't news? But nobody does anything about it, they're all part of the racket. Now I'm a Plain Man like the rest of them but a Plain Man with a voice. When I speak, they understand. Do you know those lines of Chesterton's, 'These are the people of England and they have not spoken yet?' Well, I mean to make them speak. And when they do – "

He wiped his mouth with his napkin, looked at his guest and suddenly burst out laughing.

"Don't look so serious, boy. I've got my own racket, if you like to put it that way, only mine is honest. I'm for Ocky Gaye, and if you come in with me you're for Ocky Gaye too. Shall I tell you what I say? All work corrupts, and working for Ocky Gaye corrupts completely. You have been warned."

He had been warned. That was the day on which Charles Kirton turned into Boy Kirton, which was what Ocky, and in the end everybody else, came to call him.

Chapter Two

The noise in the corridor outside, a sort of scuffling, a deep rich voice mingled with another that was higher and lighter, had an effect on them all. It was as though they were characters in some modern variation on the Sleeping Beauty fairy story, figures in whose arteries the blood was permanently frozen, whose hearts were stopped until the moment when they heard the Prince's voice. Now, as Ocky Gaye came in at the door, *burst in* as one said in the good old cliché which yet had some curious application here because something did seem to burst apart as he entered, some envelope or vacuum sealing the room from the world broke, and the four of them lived and moved again as sentient beings. After Ocky, helter skelter, came a dazed-looking girl whom he was holding, almost dragging, by the arm, his blonde secretary Mercury Ellis, and Bill Stead, who edited the Complaints section of the paper which was called "Plain Words from our Readers." Bill Stead was in his mid-twenties, a young man of enamelled elegance normally uncrackable. There was a faint residual native accent in his voice, but in dress and manner Bill was one of those Americans who like to appear more English than the English. Ocky was in the full flight of speech.

"I came in and I found Jeannie, Jeannie Cameron here, down in that picturesque mass of fake marble we call a reception hall, just pushing open one of the exit doors and crying. Leaving Plain Man Enterprises with tears running down her pretty face. You're not crying now, are you, my dear?"

She shook her head. The marks of tears were still on her cheeks. She was in her teens, and in fact she was not pretty.

"And why do you think she was crying? Because she'd come to the Plain Man and been turned away. Told her story was of no interest."

"I thought – " Bill Stead began, and was cut short.

"You don't think, you haven't the apparatus. Tell them your story, Jeannie, tell them what you told me." He gave Mercury Ellis, who had been examining her nails, a great smack on the buttocks. "Pay attention."

She recited monotonously, "There are seven of us in two rooms. Mum and Dad and five children. I'm the eldest, I'm seventeen. Rickie's fourteen, Mary's thirteen, and the twins are only four. There's no water in the flat, the sink's out on the landing, and the toilet's two floors below and only one for the whole house. And we pay two pounds five a week."

"And your landlord, just tell them about him."

"He owns a lot of houses, so they say, and he charges like that in all of them. And the roof leaks. His name's Mr Emanuel."

"And, and, and, and."

"He's trying to get us out."

"Come on now, come on. And?"

She whispered the most shameful thing of all. "He's a black man."

"Of course it's terrible," Bill Stead said. "There are lots of cases like this, and they're all terrible, but it's possible to get these injustices put right through..." His voice, with its American accent showing strongly in this moment of stress, faded away under Ocky's baleful glare.

"I didn't bring you here to be told how injustices can be put right." Big head thrust forward, he suddenly shouted, "Did you happen to know that this slum landlord has threatened that if Jeannie or any of her family go to the police or make any sort of complaint to anybody they'll be cut – and not only the mother and father but the little kids, the twins? Did you know that?"

Stead shook his head, overwhelmed. "You didn't take the trouble to find out. You just listened to Jeannie's story for a couple of minutes and then you were ready to send her away, am I right?"

Stead made a strangled noise that might have meant anything. Ocky's voice suddenly became calm and mellifluous, the voice with which he charmed television audiences.

"I can forgive a mistake, but I can't forgive a failure of human sympathy. Mercury, see that he gets a month's pay cheque. Goodbye, Bill."

He held out his hand, a sweet forgiving smile on his lips. Stead gripped the hand as though it were magnetised, turned, left the room.

"Now, Jeannie, you just sit down and I'll tell you what's going to happen." He placed the girl in a chair, where Dex, Jimmy, Boy and Francie looked at her rather as though she were some specimen of a new, unlikeable human type. "You're going home in a car, you understand that, and you're going to put everybody into that car, Mum and Dad and Richie and Mary and the twins. You're going to spend tonight at a hotel, and on Friday you're going on to my television programme, and you're going to tell the exact story of the way you've been living, do you understand?"

She looked up at him adoringly, nodded. Francie moved one leg over another, a rustling of silk.

He might have been telling a story to a child. "And after that, you're never going back to those two rooms. The Plain Man is going to find you a house to live in, a house where you won't be worried by people like Mr Emanuel. Will you like that?"

She began to cry again. "You're so kind."

Generosity fairly glowed out of his broad face, shone in his blue eyes, dripped from his stubby hands. "It's what we're here for, to help people like you. Mercury, you take Jean along to Ray Pillin. Tell him what I want. She's to go down to my car, and Ray's to go with her and take pictures. He'd better take a couple of the boys in case of trouble." He lifted Jean from her chair, planted upon her forehead an avuncular kiss.

They watched her follow Mercury out. Then Jimmy Crundle, who handled the television programme said, "I don't know, Chief, I'm not sure I like it. Negroes are plain men too. You go on the air and slam negro landlords and they'll be saying you're anti-negro, talking about the colour bar and all that."

Ocky beamed upon them, sat down. "So what? The family's being victimised. What do we do about it, nothing?"

"I just say take it easy about negroes, that's all. And the programme's been changed to Thursday this week, remember? Friday they're showing football."

"Thursday, Friday, it's all the same." Ocky waved a hand.

Boy Kirton had gone over to the window again. From there, looking down at the poster, craning his neck to see St. Paul's, he asked, "How do we find them a house?"

"I don't know, buy one, charge 'em a bit of rent. For God's sake, something like this drops in our lap, we ought to use it." He got up, walked up and down the big room, patted Francie's shoulder, said to Jimmy, "Don't worry about the negro angle, we'll find a way to do it. What do you say, Boy?"

"I say Jimmy's right."

"That's my Boy. I can tell you he's bloody well wrong. We're against slum landlords, not the negroes as people."

"Chief, I've got a paper to get out." It was Dex's editorial whine. "Have a look at these covers, will you? I don't mind telling you I'm worried about the trend of – "

The whine died away. Ocky glanced at the covers. "Make up your own mind, Dex, what are you here for? Aren't you satisfied with the covers?"

"Coverwise they're fine. I'm just wondering."

Mildly Ocky said, "What are you wondering?"

"About the church. A lot of our readers are not going to like this. And the way we're presenting it makes the whole thing worse."

"Is the circulation keeping up, Dex?" The voice was still mild, but Dex flinched as though a hot iron had been brought near to his face.

"Yes. We've gained over thirty thousand in the last six months."

"Then that shows people aren't hating us too much, don't you think? But you're the editor. If you don't like these, scrub them. Put in another feature this week. It the circulation keeps up, that'll be fine. Understand?"

Dex said nothing. He gathered up the proofs and went out.

Francie spoke for the first time since Ocky had come into the room. "What's wrong, Ocky?"

"Wrong?" He glared at her, then smiled. "I like my editors to make up their own minds, that's all. Did you want me, Jimmy?"

"It was about Thursday's programme."

"We'll have to recast it to include Jeannie Cameron. Come in at five o'clock and we'll talk about it."

Jimmy nodded and went out. When he had gone, Francie said, "Well?"

There was an understanding between these two, Boy Kirton thought, an understanding compounded of hostility and love. It was long ago, or not so very long ago but before Boy Kirton's time, that Francie had been Ocky's mistress. A different Francie Lake looked out from one of the photographs on the wall, a photograph that showed Ocky holding in his right hand a copy of the first issue of *The Plain Man*. He was laughing, and his left arm was round the shoulders of Bill Wentworth, the paper's first editor, who had died of drink or of some obscure sort of disappointment. Wentworth was laughing too, they were all laughing, including the woman on Ocky's other side, who was simply not recognisable as the well-polished, narrow-beaked bony Francie Lake of these days. It was a girl who stood laughing there, her arm round Ocky's waist, a girl laughing as they all were at the immense joke of being alive and cocking a snook at the wooden puppets, the lack-lustre nonentities, all the frauds and fakes of the world. That, at least, was the way in which Boy Kirton, who had perhaps a romantic turn of mind, chose to see it. He believed that the Francie Lake of those days no longer existed. Whether the Ocky Gaye who had started *The Plain Man* still existed, about that he was not so sure. But he knew that when Francie stubbed out a cigarette, put her thin red-clawed fingers on the desk and said "Well," she had understood something that was not clear to the rest of them, something that she had sensed as soon as Ocky entered the room.

She said positively, "You've seen Deacon."

He patted the Epstein head, nodded, smiled. "Yes."

"Well?"

He was staring at her now, and it seemed that he might break into laughter at any moment. "He's not coming in."

Chapter Three

There was silence. This is it, Boy Kirton thought, this is what it was all about, all that business of the girl, it was simply a device to put off breaking the bad news. Or not *simply*, there was nothing simple about Ocky, but *partly.* Just how bad the news was he did not know, perhaps nobody knew except Ocky and the accountants who handled the financial side of things. Perhaps nobody at all knew, not even Ocky. How much money was made by Plain Man Enterprises, where the backing came from or even whether there was any backing at all, Boy Kirton didn't know. At different times several names had been mentioned as Ocky's backers, in particular the name of Sir James Jeavons, a rich, retired industrialist who had identified himself with *The Plain Man* as a paper and as a movement. But Jeavons had been dead for nearly a year. In the last few months it had been generally understood (and this meant, perhaps, no more than that Ocky had assiduously dropped and placed stories in the Press) that Dan Deacon, Sir Daniel Deacon, who had made a fortune out of speculative building, was eager to have a share in a magazine empire, and that he would buy a share of Plain Man Enterprises.

It had been rumoured also that Deacon was thinking of starting a new daily paper, an enterprise that would strain the richest man's resources, and that he might appoint Ocky as editor. Certainly Deacon and his wife had been frequent visitors at the parties Ocky gave in his house at Finchley. What did it mean? Kirton didn't bother to speculate, simply accepted these stories as indications of the prevailing wind. Now it seemed that the wind had stopped blowing, and evidently Francie Lake knew all about it. That was not surprising, even though the girl in the photograph no longer existed. The surprising thing was that Boy Kirton, rather than Dex or Jimmy, should have been chosen to receive the news with her.

Ocky took off his jacket, flung it on to a chair, began to walk with quick short paces up and down the room, snapping his braces – braces that had on them a pattern of girls fleeing from young men – and talking rapidly in the voice which could flow like oil or flare like a bellows-blown fire, but was now rapid, classless, unemphatic.

"Five weeks we've been talking, haggling, bitching over details, how many per cent of this and how many per cent of that. Christ, I said, if you leave me the editorial control you can have all the financial control you want, Dan, I'm not interested in money as long as it's there. We've got to the point where we're sending in the accountants, batteries of them, and today what does he say? He doesn't like the tone of *The Plain Man* and he wants complete control."

"Editorial, too?"

"I said complete control. Must have it, he say. His advisers tell him that blah, blah, blah. Don't try to get inside your adviser's trousers, I said to him, they're not big enough, tell me straight out what you mean, and what he means is that he wants the lot." He mimicked the Welsh lilt of Deacon's voice. "My advisers tell me, you see, that the paper smells too much of Fascism, we'll have to change all that. Fascism, I ask you. We're trying to get the Government to act about the roads and the railways and about cases like Jeannie Cameron's, and he calls it Fascism."

Boy Kirton looked past the Epstein head of Ocky, as he stood snapping his braces. The head had been done years ago, it had never been literally faithful, Ocky had got a lot fatter, but you could still see beneath the squashy nose and the double chin the power and vitality that must have appealed to Epstein.

"Why don't you do what he wants?" That was Francie.

"Give up, you mean?"

"Deacon's a sort of radical, isn't he? And you'd still be editor."

"Until he liked to turn me off, and that might be any day. I can't go back, Francie. Even if I wanted to, I couldn't go back." He looked at her now in a way that was oddly appealing.

"You're up the creek, and the farther you go the narrower the passage gets. At least, that's what they tell me. Is this what you wanted me for, to break the bad news."

"I wanted your advice. You think I ought to settle with Deacon?"

"You don't want my advice. I used to think you might take notice of what I said. Now I know better."

He moved over and kissed her cheek. "I've always valued what you tell me, you know that."

"If Deacon's out of it "couldn't you get another backer? Is that impossible?" She was staring at him now, very directly.

He patted her shoulder. "We'll see. Thanks, Francie."

Boy Kirton had a sense, when she had gone, that some sort of drama had been played out, a drama whose meaning he did not fully understand. There had been surely some subterranean implications in Ocky's manner – and why had he wanted a witness to the scene? But now he pressed the button that brought the great cocktail bar, gleaming with mirrors and bottles, gliding out from the wall. He poured two large whiskies, gestured towards the bar.

"Vulgar, I expect. Would you say it was vulgar, Boy?"

"Since you ask me, yes."

"Trouble is, you know, I can't see it. I like bright colours, things you can notice. And why not, can you tell me why not? You wear clothes, why shouldn't you be noticed in them?" He flexed the braces, and the ladies on them shivered. "You're putting in a cocktail bar, what's the matter with letting people notice it? Don't answer, I know I'm wrong. But there are millions like me, that's the point, millions of people are wrong too. I represent them, that's what Francie's forgotten, though she used to know it. That's why they love me, Boy. I do the sort of things they dream about, I'm *them*. They'd like to be pouring whisky from their own cocktail bar like this, at half-past three in the afternoon." There seemed nothing to be said. Kirton sipped his whisky. "I'm not going back, Boy. If I let Deacon take over and stay on as editor it's a step back, you can't say anything else. You take one step back and it turns into three. You do that once or twice and – wham, you're just not there any more, you've disappeared. For me there won't ever be any going back."

Boy Kirton squinted at his whisky, amber against the light. Ocky went on talking.

"Deacon's played a dirty trick, stringing me along this far till he thinks I've got to accept his terms. But he's wrong, he'll come in on *my* terms." The buzzer sounded on his desk. Ocky bounded across to it.

"Didn't I tell you I was busy, you stupid bitch, didn't I say I want no, N-O, calls put through?" A confused gabbling emerged. Ocky said sweetly, "You understand now, then." He picked up a chair opposite Boy Kirton, turned it round, straddled it. "He has to come in."

"What do you mean?"

"How much do you know about Deacon?"

"Not much. He started operations in the twenties, is that right, with a small firm of his own. Then he – "

"Listen." Ocky's face was so close to his that he could see the graining of the fat cheeks that seemed, in spite of their puffiness, to be solid as marble. "I want to know everything about Deacon that there is to be known. How he was brought up, who his parents were, what his first job was, why he left it, how his firm got started, and from there on the whole history, what he likes to eat, who he sleeps with, whether his wife knows about it."

"You want me to ask?"

"He's got servants, hasn't he? Find one who's been sacked, get them to talk. And I want all the details of his present set-up, everything. I want to know the sort of things about him that Deacon's forgotten." He broke off, grinned. "You know what I mean."

It was at times like this, and there had been three or four of them in the years he had been with Ocky, that the whisky in Boy Kirton's mouth tasted like bilgewater, and that he wanted to get up, walk out of the room and never come back. It was not exactly out of fear that he had refrained from doing so – not at all out of fear, he told himself – but because he had himself become too deeply involved in what he might have called, when he was at Oxford, a Nietzschean interpenetration of good and evil. Begin with the assumption that Ocky Gaye was a good thing, that he was the sort of individualistic force badly needed as a corrective to the bureaucrats and money-grabbing speculators of modern Britain – and it was this assumption that those who worked for Ocky always made, however mixed might be their motives in making it – and you were led inevitably to agree that there were times when you had to preserve this force by playing things dirty. Either you played it dirty or you gave up, and the fact that Ocky never gave up was one of the things you admired in him. After a time you ceased to question, perhaps even ceased to notice, the interpenetration, you no longer asked yourself whether stunts like the one with Jeannie Cameron were justifiable, but accepted them as part of Ocky's struggle against injustice. Then, every so often, you were brought up with a jolt against something like this, and you wanted to walk away.

"You don't like it."

"No."

"But you'll do it."

He replied as though it had been a question. "Yes."

Ocky put an arm round his shoulders. He was the sort of exuberant little man whom you would expect to smell powerfully of sweat, but Ocky did not smell at all and Boy Kirton, who for years now had disliked any sort of physical contact with other human beings, felt nothing disagreeable, nothing but an emotional warmth, in the light touch of this arm. "He's got to come in, Boy. Too many people know about this. I can't let him off the hook."

"There are other fish."

The arm was removed, Ocky began to walk up and down again, throwing sentences or parts of them over his shoulder. "It's too late. I told you, too many people know. I'm in a spot."

"You're always in a spot." He smiled as he said this, and it was true that there was always a libel action to be settled or a petty blackmailer to be paid off. Ocky grinned back at him.

"This time it's a real spot. You wouldn't want to see old Ocky dragged through the Bankruptcy Court now, would you? I'm not kidding, you know. Can you imagine it – old Ocky in the Bankruptcy Court?" At this point the humour of the idea was too much for him, and he began to laugh with such unaffected enjoyment that Boy Kirton laughed too. He was at the door when Ocky pressed down a switch on his intercom, winked at him, held up a hand.

A voice said, "Stead."

Ocky raised his voice to a melodious boom. "Bill Stead? Are you still there, didn't I say goodbye to you?"

The voice said something confusedly. Ocky cut it short.

"Bill, I was angry. I said things I shouldn't have done, I want to say now that I'm sorry."

The voice was apologising, abjectly. Ocky let it run to a close this time.

"Bill, let's forget the goodbye, and say hallo again tomorrow morning. Just one more thing."

The voice said eagerly, "Yes?"

"Have you collected that cheque from Mercury?"

"Yes."

"Then tear it up. Tear it up now let me hear you doing it." He fairly rocked with laughter. "My word, if you'd cashed that cheque it really would have been goodbye."

He pushed up the switch, sat down behind his desk, took out a gold toothpick and probed with it among his teeth. The face he presented to Kirton was serious, pompous, a statesman's face. "Everything, Boy, everything."

Chapter Four

Superficially the employees of Plain Man Enterprises resembled those of any other magazine group, but there was some quality in their relationship with Ocky Gaye that, among those who had been associated with him for a length of time, affected their whole lives, so that their private existences showed certain unusual features.

Dexter Welcome, for instance, lived with his third wife in a flat just off Maida Vale. He drank a great deal, and they quarrelled about this. After one more than usually violent quarrel, Marian Welcome had attacked Dexter with a frying pan. She wielded this humdrum weapon with such effect that he was knocked down and suffered slight concussion. Marian then collapsed, and had to be taken to a mental home, where she stayed for three months. She was out of the home now and they were together again, but Dexter came home drunk two or three evenings a week, and they were again quarrelling violently.

Jimmy Crundle lived with his wife and their three children in a piece of stockbroker's Tudor just outside Esher. He was in most ways an exemplary husband, and was no more than a moderate drinker. There were occasions, however, when under the influence of drink Jimmy was subject to fits of manic violence.

At an office party he had tried to rape a girl, punching her in the face and splitting her lip when she offered resistance, and in the bar of the *British Volunteer,* the pub almost next door to the office, he had knocked down a man, kicked him when he lay on the ground, and broken two of his ribs. On each occasion Ocky had come to the rescue, and had saved Jimmy from prosecution, by heavy cash payments to the girl's parents, and to the man. Jimmy had been deeply repentant, but his wife was in dread that there would be a third outbreak, in circumstances that permitted no cash settlement.

Francie Lake had a flat in a house just off Baker Street. She lived alone in this flat. She exercised a tight control over her emotions, and few people in the office knew much about her private life. Boy Kirton had been astonished to meet her one evening, with a man much younger than herself, at a rather expensive night club. She had merely nodded, and had not referred to the occasion afterwards.

Boy Kirton also lived alone, on the fourth floor of a modern block in Chelsea. He had done so ever since the death of his wife in a car accident four years ago. He occasionally brought girls to this flat, but the results were never very satisfactory. One girl had suggested that she should move in and live with him, a suggestion he had refused with shuddering impoliteness.

These four case histories could be expanded into a dozen. It did not appear to any of the people involved that there was anything unusual about their lives. Dex would have agreed that he didn't get on with his wife, Jimmy Crundle admitted that occasionally he went off the rails, Francie Lake said that she had had enough of men. Of the four, only Boy Kirton might have felt inclined to analyse the curious loneliness of Ocky Gaye's chief executives, might have realised that their lives were split in two, and might have concluded that their connection with Ocky and Plain Man Enterprises had been developed at the expense of their private lives. From this psychological maladjustment, if that is what it was, Ocky himself seemed immune. His first wife, Angela, had run away with a French sailor, but his second wife, Claire, presided very competently over the big dinner parties he gave, at which the guests were principally politicians, actors and actresses, and television personalities. Among the people connected with Plain Man Enterprises, Ocky Gaye was the only one who appeared to live a fully integrated and settled life.

On the day after he had talked to Ocky, Kirton passed over the routine work of *Crime Today* to Jack Smedley, and began to dig. He knew, without being told, that this was not the sort of job that could be given to a detective agency or trusted to any subordinate, that Ocky wanted it done personally and secretly. He spent two or three hours following Deacon's life as it appeared in a newspaper library's cuttings, and after that talked to a little Fleet Street hanger-on known, because of his insinuating skill in discovering scandal, as Wormy Jinks. He drew a blank. Wormy knew of nothing against Deacon. Was there anything queer about his early days in Cardiff? Not that Wormy knew. The little man looked at Kirton slyly. "Your governor wouldn't want to go in with anyone who wasn't respectable, right?"

"I don't know about that."

"I've remembered a name, now. I'm not saying there's anything in it, but there might be. But there's no taste in nothing, is there?"

Kirton had already given him a ten shilling note. He handed over another.

"It's worth more than that if it's worth anything at all, but I never could keep my trap shut. There's an old school friend of Deacon's at Cardiff who was with him when he started out. His first partner he was, so I believe. Name's Dai Jenkins. I believe he could tell you some tales."

"Is that all, Wormy? I don't call it much for a quid."

"It's all I know." The little man shrugged. "See you."

It wasn't much but when, after drawing some more blanks in London, he went down on the following day to Cardiff he went to see Dai Jenkins, and told him that he was writing an article on Sir Daniel Deacon for a weekly paper. Jenkins was a long-nosed reticent man in his fifties, and he answered questions mostly in monosyllables. Yes, they had started out together, he and Dan Deacon, an ironmongery business. It hadn't done too well. Deacon had bought him out and six months later had sold the business at a profit.

"You weren't too pleased about that, I dare say."

"Pleased or not, what would be the use?"

"You didn't feel he'd cheated you?"

Jenkins stared. "No, he was smart, you see, that's what Dan Deacon was, too smart for me, but I bear him no grudge for that, man."

"Would you say he was the sort of man nobody bore a grudge against?"

"I wouldn't say that, not of anybody. Is it one of those scandal sheets you're writing for?"

"We've got to present an overall picture."

After a tedious half-hour he got the names of half a dozen people who might be able to help him, and spent the day in visiting them. It was six o'clock in the evening when he found the cottage of Jones the Milk, one of a long row in the village of Llanathly. Jones the Milk, another school friend of Deacon's, was as ruddily voluble as Jenkins had been palely saturnine. He and Dan had certainly been friends, said this small barrel of a man, that was so, yes, and wasn't it wonderful now that a journalist should come down from London to Llanathly to ask about him. Boy Kirton sat in the parlour and drank tea and listened to Jones the Milk and his wife Pat talking about what a smart boy Dan had been and the things he'd said and the way he'd been determined to get to the top. He sat and looked and smelled a smell that was partly the stuffiness of a small room and partly drains and partly the warm rich human smell of Jones the Milk and his wife. It was a smell that made him feel sick, and he was just about to go when Pat, who was a roly-poly, suety counterpart of her husband, said, "It's sad that Gwyneth can't be here to listen. She'd have something to say about Dan Deacon."

"Ah, she'd have something to say," Jones the Milk nodded.

"That's our daughter, Gwyneth, I'm meaning. Pretty as a doll she was, hair like the ripe corn when she was a kid and Dan Deacon a young man, she worshipped him, would have kissed the ground he trod on."

"She's married now?"

"In the asylum," Jones the Milk said placidly.

"The asylum?"

"She was always a little bit touched, the gift of God they call it, seeing visions and dreaming dreams. There were times she thought Dan was the Archangel Gabriel come down from Heaven to bring her the love of God. She was a wild one, even before her time."

"What time?"

Barrel and pudding exchanged glances. "You'll not use this in your paper."

"Of course not."

"She was taken off when she was fifteen. Thirty-two years ago it was this year." He paused. Kirton said nothing, waited for the story to unfold. "Before she was taken, she said that Dan Deacon had been with her."

"It was not true, Willy, you know it was not true," pudding protested.

"Have I said it was true, now? Did I ever say a word about believing it?"

"It's not what you say, Willy Jones, it's the manner that you say it, and is it the sort of thing you should be talking of to strangers?"

"Stranger, damn, he's a journalist," said Jones the Milk. "And why did she come in weeping that night then, weeping and with her clothing torn and telling us the tale she did?"

"Willy Jones," pudding cried, her face bright red. "You know well she wasn't in her right mind, nor had been for a twelve-month."

He tapped fat finger into fat palm. "And why does Dan give money for her support, then, and has done thirty years and more, will you tell me that?"

Boy Kirton sat back, tried to forget that warm rich sweaty smell, and listened to them arguing, but he heard little more. On an August night thirty-two years ago Gwyneth Jones, who was known as a wild one in Llanathly, a girl who had the gift of God and did not behave as other people, had come in crying, with her clothing torn, and had said that Dan Deacon had been with her. Dan Deacon had denied it, perhaps nobody had fully and truly believed it, but it had been after this night that Gwyneth's wavering mental balance tipped over into psychosis. Ever since that time Dan Deacon, who had just a year or two earlier gone into the building line, had paid for Gwyneth's upkeep in the mental home where she was a permanent inmate.

It was not much of a story, but it was better than nothing. Boy Kirton thought about the story as he drove back to Cardiff, but didn't see any way in which Ocky could use it.

He sat in the hotel lounge after his return, drinking sherry, all energy drained from his body. He closed his eyes, stuck out his legs, put his hands close to sides, the palms touching thighs. So the dead lay on tombs, in effigy – or of course with hands folded over the breast. It was while he was wondering whether to change the position of his hands that he heard Ocky's voice, opened his eyes and sat up, the dead restored. "Octavius Gaye's Half Hour" had just begun, and the door of the television room was open. He was sucked in, as stuff is by a vacuum cleaner.

The preliminaries, the calypso about Ocky fighting for truth and justice, the shot of him looking grave and statesmanlike, were over. Ocky was opening his correspondence, reading the letters aloud. The second one came from the parents of a naval cadet who had run away from his unit. His parents said that the boy had complained time and again that he was being bullied. Ocky looked immensely stern, pushed a button on his desk. Dex Welcome came in. Ocky tapped the letter.

"Action," he said, "I want *action* on this." Now Ocky disappeared and *action* ensued on the little screen, a hectic melée or melange or mish-mash of telephone calls and button-pressing and people scurrying down corridors saying "Just a moment while I – " and "It's the case of Cadet Willis I want to talk about," and "Cadet Willis, yes, I think we've – " There was a positive furore of cross-cutting between places vaguely recognisable (or perhaps they weren't recognisable, it didn't matter) as *The Plain Man* offices, the Admiralty, some sort of training ship. There were four boys yanked out of their sleeping quarters by petty officers, and paraded in a square before what seemed to be a whole naval unit. There was Cadet Willis, one supposed it was Cadet Willis, marching smartly up to an officer and saluting. A fanfare of trumpets. A stentorian voice saying, "The *action* achieved involved the punishment of the bullies and the reinstatement of Cadet Willis."

Back to Ocky, smiling benevolently now. "So you see it's not impossible for justice to be done. In fact, I don't mind telling you that I've got a lot of faith in British justice, in spite of the layers of red tape, bureaucracy and petty-mindedness in which it's so often wrapped up. It needs a plain man, sometimes, to cut through the wrappings. On this occasion I'm proud to have been the man. By the way, the story of Cadet Willis was true in every detail, but the names have been changed. We want the bullies punished, yes, but we don't want them persecuted, do we?"

That was the end of the first half of the programme. The second half, Boy Kirton knew, would be the Camerons. He watched the opening sequence, which showed Jeannie Cameron coming into the entrance hall.

"I want to see Mr Gaye, Mr Octavius Gaye."

A commissionaire said, "Mr Gaye is a very busy man, miss."

"But this is very important."

"I'm sorry, miss. Mr Gaye is out. If you care to leave a message – "

She turned away, utterly disconsolate. But who was this pushing open the great doors, bouncing into the entrance hall on little springy legs, stopping at sight of the girl who walked sadly past him head down, approaching her and putting an arm round her shoulders, his eyes milky with human kindness? Who but the Plain Man himself, Ocky Gaye...

Boy Kirton had seen enough. He left a spellbound crowd of viewers, most of them middle-aged, and went in to dinner.

Chapter Five

Ocky Gaye got out of bed every day at seven o'clock in the morning, and there did fifteen minutes' work with the Indian clubs before taking a hot bath. After the bath he ate toast and drank coffee while scanning the papers for anything useful to Plain Man Enterprises. After that Bettridge, one of his secretaries, read the personal post to him while he dressed. At eight-fifteen he kissed Claire goodbye and the chauffeur, Levitt, drove him from Finchley to the office in the Rolls. On the way he dictated to Bettridge so that his personal post was dealt with before he got to the office.

This routine was varied only when he stayed in the flat just above the office, on the pretext that he had a great deal of work that could only be done in the office but in reality, as Claire very well knew, because he wanted to sleep with a girl. There were a good many of these girls, and they had certain characteristics in common. They were always young, always plump, and always plebeian. Ocky made no secret of the fact that he had been brought up in a Stepney orphanage, abandoned by a father who had died seeking a fortune in Venezuela and a mother who had gone on the streets. He had never tried, as some do, to emancipate himself from his background, using it rather as a perfectly appropriate origin for the earnest seeker after truth who had learned French at night school, discovered a talent for street corner oratory when he was eighteen, and become finally the great Plain Man of Britain. In the morning the girl was always bustled away early, as some kind of curious concession to respectability, and Ocky breakfasted on an omelette and champagne, sent in from a neighbouring restaurant.

On the night before Boy Kirton's return from Cardiff Ocky stayed at the flat. The girl he brought up there was a Soho striptease dancer who called herself Lola Monterez. Her real name was Ethel Hulme, and she was a big girl from Lancashire. When Ocky woke, he was annoyed to see that the time was ten minutes to eight, and acutely dissatisfied to discover her by his side. The satisfactions of the night were for him never extended into the morning. Night for Ocky was the time for sex, morning for Indian clubs and dictation.

"Up," he said. "Time to get up."

She continued to sleep, a big girl, naked, her lipstick smearing the pillow. Ocky did some Swedish exercises – he kept no Indian clubs at the flat – prodded her buttocks with his hand and then pinched her. She woke with a yelp.

"Up," he said, "Up and out. Out, out, out."

She yawned. "What's the time? Christ, it's only just eight o'clock. You might let a girl sleep."

"Come on, come on, I've got work to do."

She began to laugh. "You do look funny, standing there like that. I say, you are fat."

It was true, he saw, as he looked at himself in the glass on the wall. He was a sturdy little man with short legs, a big stomach and a fine head. He scowled at the figure in the glass and put his tongue out at it. "Come on, love," she said. "Come and do some work back here. Get a bit of that weight off you."

He did as she suggested, and enjoyed it, but felt that valuable minutes were being used up. By the time Lola had got up, dressed, eaten the breakfast that was brought in by the night watchman, Hayles, and kissed him goodbye, it was after eight-thirty. He gave her twenty pounds when they parted, and spent five minutes after she had left in totting up the cost of the encounter. It had begun when, after the television show, he had taken out to dinner an American Congressman visiting England and a Cockney ex-gangster named Shivers Stewart, whose reminiscences were being ghosted for *Crime Today*. They had gone on to what Shivers Stewart assured them was the best and most discreet of striptease clubs, and he had left them with two girls, in a hotel. The evening had cost something like a hundred pounds.

He dismissed this fact from his conscious mind, but he was very snappy with Bettridge. A hundred pounds was nothing in itself, but the whole incident seemed somehow ominous. The continued existence of his paper empire often seemed to Ocky miraculous. He was aware that at the moment, so the accountant doctors said, it was a patient needing great transfusions of money, and what had he just done but *spent* money? He felt the premonitory twinges of an ulcer patient who has greedily indulged in a delicious fry, and is waiting for retribution.

For half an hour Ocky was gloomy, but his spirit was too volatile ever to be kept down for long. There were people telephoning to congratulate him on last night's show, there was Dex coming in to say it had been the best ever, there was young Bill Stead coming in to say that he'd learned a lesson last night from seeing Ocky handle the Cameron family on television.

"The human touch, Bill," Ocky said. "It's vital. And the national touch. You're American born and bred, Bill – "

"I've lived here for years," Stead protested.

"That's not the point. You've got to have sympathy and understanding inside you, in *here.*" He thumped his chest. "I'm a Cockney, the Camerons are Scots, but I understand them, I've got the human touch and the national touch, too. I sometimes wonder whether those who aren't British bred can ever have it." Stead looked dejected. "Don't take me too seriously now, Bill, I don't want you to leave us. You've got a future here. It's just that I want you to understand things as I do. This Cameron business now, it's a real live issue, the sort they pay no attention to in the talking shop, do you see that? What part of America do you come from now, Bill, the South?"

"New York."

"Ah. Anyway, the point I want to make is that I've got no objection to coloured people, neither have you, we're liberals. I'd employ them here if they applied for jobs and were competent to do them. All we're saying is that we *don't* want coloured landlords cheating white people, that *The Plain Man* won't have it. This is a live issue and it appeals to our readers, do you see that, Bill?"

Bill Stead said that he did see it. Ocky dismissed him and, in a glow of self-satisfaction, lighted his first cigar of the day. He smoked it with enjoyment, until it occurred to him to wonder how much cigars cost. Then he put it out. Boy Kirton, who had travelled up on the night train, found him staring gloomily at the extinct torpedo.

"Has it ever occurred to you, Boy, that in a decent world, a world fit for Plain Men and Women to live in, things like that cigar would cost twopence each instead of ten shillings, that anybody who wanted to would be able to enjoy the good things of this earth?"

"Do they really cost ten shillings? As much as that?"

"A figure of speech. They're luxury, that's the point. I'm giving up luxuries." He looked across at a cartoon representing him as St. George spearing the dragon of Parliamentary bureaucracy.

"I saw the show last night. I thought it really had punch."

"You did?" Ocky brightened immediately. "You were down in Cardiff, weren't you? What did you get?"

Kirton told him. When he had finished, Ocky lighted another cigar.

"Would you believe it, the old ram. Drives a girl of fifteen off her nut and then thinks he can get out of it by paying the bill. That's the Welsh for you all over, sexy and sly."

"It wasn't like that." Boy Kirton's smooth round face was troubled. "The odds are he had nothing to do with the girl at all."

"She said he'd been with her, didn't she? And he's paying for her, you told me he was."

"Yes, but – "

"Is she absolutely bonkers?" Ocky used rather affectedly old-fashioned slang at times.

"She couldn't give evidence in a court or anything like that, from what I've heard."

"How about Mum and Dad?"

"They wouldn't say anything. It seemed to me Dad, that's Jones the Milk, was a bit suspicious, but neither of them would ever say anything. They're grateful to Deacon, and on the face of it they've got cause to be. I'm just telling you the story. As far as I can see there's nothing in it."

"You've done a good job, Boy. This needs thinking about."

"Do you want me to go on digging?"

"No, no. You get back to that crime magazine baby of yours, she's crying out for you. Before you go, tell me this. You run into a cul-de-sac and three policemen are waiting for you at the open end of it, what do you do?"

"Give yourself up, I suppose."

"I don't. I try to jump over the wall."

When Boy Kirton left, Ocky was in great good humour. He lighted another cigar and smoked it down to the end. After lunch he sent for Ray Pillin, and asked Mercury Ellis to get Shivers Stewart into the office. Then he added a few dramatic touches to an article on corruption in trade unions.

Chapter Six

Beneath the thin surface respectableness of Plain Man Enterprises there bubbled a strong-smelling stream of raffish life. Dex Welcome and Jimmy Crundle and Francie Lake and Boy Kirton were a bit queer in their different ways, they did not flinch from dirtying their hands when it was necessary, but when all was said and done they belonged to that great army of the bourgeois which is shocked by – for example – the very idea of going to prison. But some of the distribution staff and sales representatives were of a harder breed.

Boy Kirton was at times quite distressed by the sort of thick-eared thug he saw hanging about in the van bays, and it was said in Fleet Street that newsagents in working-class districts who tried to cut down their order of *The Plain Man* or *Crime Today* or one of the other papers might find their windows inexplicably broken or learn that their delivery boys had met with accidents which ended with the loss or destruction of their papers. There had been few complaints to the police – one man who complained had been attacked afterwards at night by assailants he was unable to identify – and the sales of Plain Man periodicals kept up remarkably well. But all this remained officially unknown to those concerned with the editorial side, and reality was only brought right home to them when they met people like Ray Pillin in the corridors.

Ray Pillin was a little man whose wrinkled features seemed ingrained with dirt. His trousers were often frayed, and his brown shoes down at heel. He was a photographer and had been fined in the police courts three times, twice for taking indecent photographs and once for exhibitionism. On the third occasion he had been lucky to escape with a fine. Dex, Jimmy Crundle and Boy Kirton had once banded together to ask Ocky to get rid of Ray Pillin. Ocky professed indignation.

"You want me to get rid of a man just because he's been unlucky and got into a bit of trouble, what kind of democracy is that?"

"It's not only that," said Dex, who was their spokesman. "It's really that he – well, he doesn't seem to belong in the organisation."

"He's a good photographer, right?"

"Oh, he's good all right."

"He's not one of us," said Jimmy, who could never keep his mouth shut.

"Isn't he, Jimmy? Now, that's a distinction I never make. If Ray's got his little quirks, then so have the rest of us. That's the way I feel about it." Ocky said it with the utmost geniality, but they all knew that it was no more than six months ago that he had paid several hundred pounds to the parents of the girl attacked by Jimmy at the office party.

"We're a happy family, boys, and I want to keep us that way. Come to me, tell me that Ray's fallen down on a job, prove it, and he'll be out on his neck. But as for anything else, I'm sorry to think you're less broad-minded than I am."

They retired in confusion. Francie, who had refused to join the deputation, laughed when Boy Kirton told her what had happened.

"I told you it was a waste of time. While Ocky finds Ray Pillin useful, he won't get rid of him."

"How can he be useful?"

"I don't know, very likely Ocky doesn't know either. It's just that he always likes to have one or two people around equipped for" – she solemnly lowered one eyelid – "dirty work."

And so, whatever people felt, Ray Pillin sneaked softly along the corridors and took his photographs, faking them when necessary, and visited at night the sleazy little clubs where he occasionally got beaten up, and was generally ready for anything that might turn up.

"Sit down, Ray," Ocky said and he sat down, the toes of his scuffed shoes turned in slightly towards each other, his small creased face pointing inquiringly towards his master. "I've got a job for you. It's a private job, and I don't want any word of it leaking out.

"I understand, Chief." Ray's voice was very soft, and seemed full of sibilants.

Ocky was smoking another cigar. He walked up and down the office, looking occasionally out of the window at the poster, sometimes at the mementoes of his past on the wall – a letter of thanks from Ernest Bevin, a cartoon by Vicky done when he had walked out of the House of Commons, a signed photograph of Jimmy Hoffa and another of Lloyd George, tributes from half a dozen organisations on whose behalf *The Plain Man* had raised funds.

"That was a good job you did on the clergyman story. You dressed up an actor, is that right?"

"Yes. It wasn't too difficult."

"I want you to do another job like that, but this time I shall need the man picked very carefully, and the girl too."

"Getting the girl is no trouble, for a fiver you can get – "

"I didn't say I wanted you to do the picking. You'll take the pictures, that's all. There'll be a man and a girl going into a hotel, you get a picture of them going in. Not one of those hotels where they let rooms by the hour, but still one where they don't make any fuss about registrations, you know the sort of place?"

"I know half a dozen."

"Good. Now, I want a few people around when these two come in. I want their progress tracked up to the bedroom, I don't care who sees them, but the man has to be recognised by these witnesses when we show them a photograph, they must be prepared to say 'Yes, that was the man who came into my hotel.' "

"It will take some dropsy."

"Some dropsy, all you need. They go up to their rooms, you're in the corridor outside. The girl screams, opens the door. The man's attacked her, she's frightened. You're in like a knife, take your pictures, girl with her clothes torn, man undressed. Now there's trouble. The manager threatens to call the police, the man drops him ten quid to keep his mouth shut. Man and girl get dressed, leave separately. That's the end of it."

Ray rubbed his shoes together, making a noise that put Ocky's teeth on edge. "That ten quid, better make it twenty."

"All right."

"Is this for us, Chief? I mean, are we using it in one of the papers?"

"No. If it all goes through as I want, there'll be no publicity. None at all."

"I don't understand."

"You don't have to understand, Ray." Ocky came close to Ray Pillin who did not meet the gaze of his blue eyes but looked down, like a very old little boy, rubbing his shoes together uneasily. "This is important, and I'm trusting you. But if you try to cross me, I'll break you. I'll have you inside before you know what hit you. I can do it, you know that, don't you?"

Ray Pillin nodded, still looking shyly down, reluctant to acknowledge that there had been occasions other than those three that everybody knew about, occasions when Ocky had saved him from quite certain imprisonment at the price only of a mere signed factual record. Like a small boy still he muttered, "I just wanted to know, that's all." Then he looked at Ocky and it was not a small boy at all, but a little, wicked, dirty old man who was staring up at him.

"It's better that you shouldn't understand. I want you to fix the hotel and the witnesses, that's all."

"Yes. And I can tell them positively that there'll be no publicity? It makes a difference."

"I want them to say what they saw, I want it down on paper, but otherwise there'll be no publicity."

"The man and the girl, will they know that I'm going to take pictures."

"Yes, they'll know. One more thing about the pictures. I shall want them quickly after the job's done. How soon can I have them?"

"A couple of hours. You want me to bring them to you?"

"I'll let you know when the time comes. And that won't be long. I can't tell you exactly when this will come off, but it will be soon."

It was Ocky's belief that in an enterprise of this sort you halved the risk rather than doubling it by involving several people. To have entrusted the whole operation to Ray Pillin, for example, would have been to invite disaster, and, in spite of the hold that he retained over Ray, even the possibility of blackmail. The affair had already involved Boy Kirton and Ray Pillin. It was to embrace also Shivers Stewart, Francie Lake, and such executants as the man and woman who were to enact the scene in the hotel. Ocky expected, and surprisingly often got, absolute faithfulness in those who worked for him, but still it was just as well that none of these people should have a complete picture of what was to happen.

There was one other person who would be brought into the affair, a very old friend of Ocky's named Joe Mycock. Ten years ago Joe Mycock had been a promising middle-weight boxer, and Ocky, who had dabbled in most things, held a half interest in him. Joe was quick, and had a volcanically violent right hand. His hopes of becoming anything more than promising were ended when, in a fight with the European champion, the skin over both his eyes was badly split, and he had to retire. The skin healed, and Joe Mycock had half a dozen more fights, in every one of which his eyes were cut. When the cuts affected his sight, and two operations became necessary, Ocky paid all the bills. He looked after Joe's family while he was in hospital and when he came out, with his sight saved but his vision permanently affected, Ocky gave him a pension for life as well as sending him an enormous food hamper every Christmas. There was nothing at all that Joe Mycock, a moderately honest man, would not have done for Ocky Gaye.

Chapter Seven

The telephone call came on Tuesday morning, while Dan Deacon was eating breakfast. Hilda, the very competent German girl who ran their house in St. John's Wood, took the call and came into the breakfast room.

"There is a man on the telephone who wishes to speak to you."

"Who is it?"

"He does not say his name."

Deacon put down his napkin, went into the living room. His wife Bella could hear his voice, but not the words he was saying. He came back in a couple of minutes, sat down again, buttered himself a piece of toast. She looked up from the paper.

"Who was it, dear?"

"Nothing."

"But it must have been something."

"Fellow wanted me to subscribe to some charity."

Bella Deacon could hear the edge of irritation in her husband's voice, and she did not pursue the subject. It was almost twenty-five years ago that Dan Deacon, an up-and-coming youngish building contractor, had married the daughter of a country doctor. She had borne him three children, they had more money than she ever knew what to do with, and they had also the small house in St. John's Wood and a large one in Hampshire, a yacht, three motor-cars. Above all, they had happiness, possessed it so firmly that it almost seemed to Bella

Deacon that she held this abstraction in her hands, could touch and smell it. What she felt for the husband who had given her everything she could have wished for from life was more than love and respect, it was something like worship. The deepest perturbations of her life were concerned with the heart condition aggravated by her tendency to eat too much through sheer pleasure, and so to put on weight. She returned to her bacon and egg, feeling faint stirrings of alarm only when her husband pushed away his toast.

"What is it, Dan? Aren't you feeling well?"

"I'm quite all right."

She returned to the paper but saw him, a moment or two later, looking absently out of the window. That, too, was uncharacteristic.

"What is it, Dan?"

"I told you it was nothing." He got up, dabbed at his lips, went into the hall. "I'm not sure what time I shall be back this evening, I've got one or two appointments."

"But you'll be in to dinner?"

"If not, I'll let you know." He kissed her.

She watched him as he left the house, taking pride in the erect lean handsomeness topped by a bowler hat, thinking that he looked much less than his sixty years. He was walking to the office, as he often did. There he would work, accumulate money, come home again. She sighed with pleasure at the thought of it, and at the thought of her three handsome sons, one in his last term at Oxford, the two others at Winchester. Happiness made her feel hungry. She looked at the hot-plate and saw with pleasure that there was another egg.

Deacon walked to his office in the lucid October sunlight, and as he walked thought about the telephone call, a call which had puzzled rather than alarmed him. He was, however, conspicuously brusque that day, and was snappish even to his devoted secretary Miss Brocklebank. He frowned when she presented him with the list of his engagements.

43

"Seven o'clock John Adderton. Who made that appointment? And who is John Adderton?"

"He's a partner in a firm that runs one of those pension schemes for executives. You couldn't see him earlier."

"Why should I see him? It's a matter for our accountants."

"You said you were interested, and would like to see him yourself." Miss Brocklebank was distressed. It was not like DD to be forgetful. Now that she had reminded him that he had made the arrangement himself, no doubt he would smile. She was quite dazzled by his smile.

DD did not smile. He simply said, "He'd better see Whyte-Jones."

She said hesitantly that she believed Mr Whyte-Jones had an engagement that evening, and DD fairly glared at her, snatched up the telephone, spoke to Mr Whyte-Jones and made him put off the engagement so that he could see Mr Adderton. The whole thing was unlike DD and it upset her.

Sir Daniel Deacon worked in his office until nearly half-past six. Much of the work he did consisted of telephone calls of a kind that puzzled Miss Brocklebank. Then he took up his bowler hat, gave her a curt good night, and left. He walked to the nearest Underground station and took a ticket for Colindale.

The little man who, on the instructions of Shivers Stewart, had been watching the building the whole afternoon, was close behind Sir Daniel when he booked a ticket. The little man himself bought a ticket to Charing Cross. There he got out and made a telephone call to say that Deacon was on his way to Colindale. Later that evening he collected a fiver from Shivers. It was a fiver easily earned and the little man, who was a professional like most of the other people engaged in the operation, promptly forgot about the whole thing.

Deacon followed the instructions he had been given on the telephone. He turned left out of the station, and walked down three streets of red brick, semi-detached houses. Several men wearing the uniform of bowler hat, dark suit and umbrella had got off the train with him and, in the darkness of the evening he was not a conspicuous figure. He stopped before a house precisely similar in its aspect to all the others, and rang the bell. Joe Mycock opened the door almost immediately. "I've sent the family out," he said. "Told them I wanted to have a bit of a private discussion like, naming no names of course. Come into the lounge."

In the small room to which he was led, with its three-piece suite, its lighting fitting shaped like a small spray of flowers, its fireplace in three differently coloured tiles, and its wild geese flying about the walls, Deacon saw a shambling figure, slab-faced and broken-nosed, with slit eyes set in puffy flesh, who smiled at him apologetically.

"Sit down and take a weight off your feet, Sir Daniel," Joe Mycock said. "I thought you might like a bit of fire, the evenings are getting chilly." He was a little awed by the presence in his house of a man with a handle to his name, and in spite of devotion to Ocky he did not like what he was doing.

Deacon did not sit down. He put his hat and umbrella on a table and then stood in the middle of the room staring at Mycock, an impressive figure with narrow head topped by curling grey hair, wide thin mouth turning down at the corners, wiry body. "You didn't give your name on the telephone. What is it?"

"My name's neither here nor there, Sir Daniel. I wish you'd sit down."

"I had inquiries made, had someone consult the electoral register. Your name is Joseph Mycock, and you were a professional boxer, now retired. What is your interest in Gwyneth Jones?"

"Wish you'd sit down," Joe Mycock grumbled and sat down himself, looking somehow absurdly out of place in the rust-coloured armchair. "And have a drink. No reason why we shouldn't talk friendly."

Deacon looked at his watch. "I'll give you five minutes. What is your interest in Gwyneth Jones?"

"What's *your* interest, eh, that's a bit more to the point."

"Tell me what you mean."

"You know. I mean to say, she was only fifteen. Everyone knows she had a thing for you, maybe it wasn't your fault. But only fifteen – and you're paying for her in the place they've put her. I mean to say, it's not a nice story, you wouldn't want it to get to the papers, would you? There's some that would print it, would want to print it." Joe Mycock's voice faltered. He was doing what Ocky had told him to do, but nothing could make him like doing it, and he did it very badly.

"Why did you tell me not to let anybody know I was coming to see you?"

"It was in your own interest, see."

"What do you mean by that? Are you trying to blackmail me?"

"That's a hard word. Why don't you have a drink?" Joe Mycock began to pour himself some beer.

"Do you know a man named Gaye?" Joe almost dropped the glass. "I see you do. And I'm not asking you, I'm telling you, Gaye put you on to this. He's got a grudge against me because I wouldn't go in with him, and so he's put you up to this trick. I don't know what Gaye thinks he's playing at but I can tell you, Mycock, this is a very dangerous game for you."

"I haven't said a word about money."

"And you'd better not. I'm telling you here and now, Mycock, that anything I did for Gwyneth Jones I did because I was sorry for the girl. Her parents will say the same. And as soon as a story to any other effect appears I'll have a libel action slapped on the paper that prints it. As for you, if I hear anything more from you I shall tell the police and let them deal with you. Do you understand?"

Joe Mycock nodded. In his slow mind there stirred a feeling of shame at what he was doing. For a moment he was on the verge of admitting that Ocky Gaye had put him up to all this, and that he wanted no part of it. Then Deacon did something that was perhaps excusable, but was certainly foolish. He looked round the little room that was Joe Mycock's pride and joy, at the wild geese and the spray of lighting flowers and the vividly patterned carpet. He drew out his wallet, picked out a pound note, let it drop from his fingers.

"You don't seem to have much of a place here," he said. "Perhaps that's your trouble. Here's a pound note."

He nodded, picked up hat and umbrella, walked out of the house. Joe Mycock sat staring at the note on the carpet with a mounting feeling of rage that he knew to be bad for him. He rose, picked up the note and threw it into the fire. Then he felt better.

Dan Deacon felt that he had carried off an awkward situation successfully. He walked to the station, took the Underground train back, and arrived home at nearly nine o'clock. When Bella gently said that he had promised to let her know if he was going to be late, he laughed, apologised, kissed her. He opened a bottle of champagne, she took a cold chicken out of the refrigerator, and by the end of their little supper party they were both feeling really rather gay.

Chapter Eight

When the little man made his telephone call to Shivers Stewart, the rest of the plan went into operation. At ten minutes to seven, on this Tuesday evening, a cab stopped outside the Eugene Hotel, which is in a street just off Westbourne Terrace, and a man and a girl got out. The man wore a bowler hat and carried an umbrella. His hair was grey, his head narrow, his mouth thin and wide. He wore a dark suit that was very much like Deacon's. The girl was young and her skirt, as she got out of the taxi, was up round her thighs. The man gave the taxi driver a five-shilling tip, but it was in any case unlikely that he would forget the pair who had been making love so uninhibitedly behind him.

Ray Pillin took a picture with his tiny camera as the man was paying the fare. In profile the man looked very much like Deacon, but in full face you could see that the resemblance was superficial. Both man and girl had been found by Shivers Stewart. The man was an actor named Charles Reckitts, who found it impossible to get work because he drugged, and when he drugged forgot his lines. He now scraped a living as a marijuana peddler, and was glad to do a job like this for money. The girl was a mystery, recently initiated into prostitution. She looked eighteen, but was in fact fourteen and a half years old. Shivers had not bothered to mention this fact to Reckitts.

The two went into the entrance hall where a pimply youth said indifferently that they had a room free. He gave them a key, and they walked away. They were on the first stairs when the youth called out, "You haven't registered. Got to register."

The man turned. "Put it down for me, old chap, will you? I'm in rather a hurry." The girl giggled.

"What name?"

He hesitated. "Dai Davies from Cardiff, Wales. And wife." The girl giggled again, and they went on upstairs.

On the landing a thick-set man who needed a shave came face to face with them. They went into room number eleven.

The thick-set man, who was the manager, went on his way downstairs. Ray Pillin came in at the entrance. The manager nodded. "They're in."

"Good. Now we wait."

"I'm not sure I like this. I can't have any trouble, no publicity."

"I told you there won't be any publicity."

"Then what's it all in aid of?"

"I don't know. What have you got to worry about? You're getting enough for letting us use your place, aren't you?"

"I don't know that it's worth it. This place is respectable."

Pillin used an obscene word. The pimply boy laughed.

"Do you suppose – " Pillin began and stopped.

Upstairs, thin but distinct, there came a scream. The photographer made for the stairs at a run, with the manager just behind him and the boy following. As they were going up the stairs the girl screamed again.

The door of room number eleven was open, and the girl stood in the doorway naked. There was a deep red line on her buttock. "Do you see what this bleeder wants to do, he wants to beat me."

Pillin took a shot of her. But where was the man? The manager was with him now, muttering angrily, doors were being opened along the passage. An American voice said, "Pipe down, will you, and let a man get some sleep."

"Come on, where is he?" Pillin said. The girl looked round fearfully. The man suddenly appeared from behind the door and grabbed her shoulder. He had a cane in his hand, and his eyes were wild. He's high, Pillin thought, he's high, there's going to be trouble. He quickly snapped them, not a good shot.

"Inside, inside," the manager said. He looked furious. The reception clerk stood at the top of the stairs with his mouth open. They all got inside the room. "That's enough," the manager said. "More than enough."

Reckitts suddenly grabbed the girl and thrust her down on the bed. He was wearing shirt, socks and shoes, nothing else. Pillin took shot after shot, trying to get their faces. The girl screamed again. The manager pulled Reckitts off by main force.

"Hey there," Pillin said, "Don't forget I'm taking pictures."

The girl cowered at one side of the room. There were teeth marks deep in her neck and on her shoulder.

"I said that's enough. I'm not having the police here." He said to the girl, "Put your clothes on and get out."

He held Reckitts' arms pinioned behind him. The girl, shivering with fright, picked up her clothes.

"Just a minute," Pillin said. "You're in no trouble now, he can't get free, go near him, look frightened, cry if you like. Good, good. Got it. Put on your clothes now." He had got a picture of the manager holding Reckitts while the girl cringed away from him.

She put on her clothes. Reckitts said, "It's all right, I shan't do anything, you can let go. I don't know what came over me. I'm sorry."

"Sorry," she said. "You should be kept in a bloody zoo."

"I don't know what came over me," Reckitts said again. "I really must apologise. Please release my arms."

"When she's gone." The manager asked the girl. "Are you all right?"

"I s'pose so." She looked at herself in a glass. She had certainly made a remarkably quick recovery. "Well, ta ta."

She went out. The manager released Reckitts, who put on his trousers. He was quiet enough now. "I suppose I've rather spoiled the show."

"I've got some pictures."

"The ones you wanted?"

"I don't know," Pillin said, and this was true. He suddenly remembered. "You make a fuss about turning him out, he drops you twenty quid."

"Come on, let's get it over," the manager said. "It makes me sick, all of it."

Reckitts stood fidgeting with his braces, not looking at them.

"Come on, come on," Pillin said impatiently.

"I can't quite manage it."

Pillin suddenly understood. What fool had trusted Reckitts with money, he wondered? Of course he was high as the sky. "How much is there left?"

"Five," Reckitts muttered.

The manager looked outraged. "Do you mean to say – "

"Keep your hair on." Pillin looked in his wallet. "I've got fourteen here. You'll have to wait for the other one."

"Not one, six. There's Bert. He wants a fiver."

"You'll have to wait for the six, then."

"Why should I wait ? That's not what we fixed."

Such a situation might have flustered a sensitive man. Pillin was well equipped to deal with it. He did not even get angry. "Look, somebody gave this clot twenty-five quid to settle with you and your boy, and he's blown twenty of it. I'm making up what I can out of my own pocket and leaving myself skint to do it. You'll get your other six tomorrow. That's all the money there is. If you don't like it you'll have to do the other thing."

"I wish I'd never let myself in for this caper, I know that."

"I'm sorry, I really am sorry." That was Reckitts. He picked up his cane.

"What do you say?" Pillin asked patiently.

"What can I say? I don't have any choice."

51

"That's right. Now can we get on with it, then."

Downstairs they staged quite a reasonable show, with the manager threatening to call the police and Reckitts persuading him not to do so. Pillin, who had slipped out of the room after them, got a couple of pictures. A man and woman who had come in to book a room listened to some of the argument, saw money handed over, turned tail. Reckitts, bowler-hatted and respectable, went out into the night. Ray Pillin went too. He left the Eugene Hotel at twenty minutes to eight.

Chapter Nine

At just about the time that Dan Deacon left his office for Colindale, Boy Kirton came down in the lift and went along to the *British Volunteer* for a drink. When his work in the office was done he became conscious always of a vast emptiness in his life. The work he did, the pure mechanics of it, the art of trimming and shaping material about the facts of crime to fit the taste of readers, absorbed him totally, but when the work was finished, what could be done with the rest of the day? There were theatres and cinemas, but they bored him more and more each year. There were books, but he found that he could never stay alone long enough to read them. There was food, but nowadays he found himself eating more and more quickly, so that he should be in time to keep some imaginary appointment. At one time he had played a good deal of tennis and squash, but in the last year or two it had seemed that he really could not spare time to play games. There was sex, but he found himself debarred from all but the most casual sexual engagements by distaste for the emotional intimacy implied in physical contact. And there was drink, which cancelled for a time the knowledge of emptiness. He rarely got drunk, but he drank a good deal.

There were two or three office groups in the bar, and he joined the one that contained Dex, Francie, Bill Stead, and a dark girl who was introduced as Bill's wife, Mary. Dex talked amusingly, as he could talk, about the problems involved in the last few issues of the paper, Ocky's changes of mind, threats of libel ingeniously turned aside, of the woman who had come in, pushed aside secretaries, assistants, executives, until finally she found her way into Dex's own office, and stared at him. "I've been looking for a Plain Man," she said, "And it looks as if I've found one." This Dex, lubricated by drink, a self-confident and cynically amused man of the world, was hardly recognisable as the nervous whiner in Ocky's office.

From her position on the bar stool which she had occupied for as long as Boy Kirton had been coming to the pub, Francie Lake turned her head and said, "You talk too much, Dex. There's no problem in editing the paper, no problem at all. Just do what Ocky tells you and you can't go wrong."

"I never argue with a lady, and especially I never argue with you, Francie," Dex said with determined piggy geniality.

"It doesn't matter about arguing. What matters is that you let Ocky eat you up."

"Inside the whale, am I?" Dex looked round humorously. "A tough old morsel."

"You're eaten up, consumed, a goner. You're dead, Dex, you just don't know it."

"What about you?" It was Mary Stead who spoke, and her voice was hostile.

Francie turned her dark, agonised, slightly drunken gaze to the young woman. "I died a long time ago, I'm petrified, petrified Lake you might say."

This, like Dex's story, was a joke Boy Kirton had heard before, but he had a feeling that he was missing some current of meaning beneath the level of this conversation.

"You think Bill ought to get out of it, is that what you mean?"

"It's up to Bill. Perhaps it's too late already, I don't know. Is it too late, Bill?"

"I just don't know what you're talking about." Bill Stead's handsome face was troubled. He put his hand over his wife's. Francie Lake's voice was strident.

"Just look around, Bill, and ask yourself if you want to become a zombie like the rest of us. You know what zombies are, the living dead as you might say, they're dead but they won't lie down. I saw a funny film once, years ago, wasn't meant to be, Bela Lugosi I think and the usual comic negro, and this negro you see is very much worried about the spirits of the undead that come marching out of their graves punctually at midnight you know, and every time they march out he calls out to Bela Lugosi, 'Zombies, massa boss, 'ware zombies.' That's what I say to you, Bill, 'ware zombies." She finished her drink. "I saw that film with Ocky."

She's in a state, Boy Kirton thought, somebody ought to see her home. Bill Stead said, "Ocky's been pretty nice to me, taking me on again after that boob over the Cameron girl."

"Taking you on." Her laugh was raucous as a parrot's. "Did you suppose he would let you go, a juicy morsel like you. He'll eat you up, every bit."

Mary Stead withdrew her hand from her husband's. "I'm going, Bill. Coming?"

"No." He deliberately turned his well-tailored back on her. Mary Stead thumped her glass on the bar and walked out. Nobody said anything.

It was perhaps half an hour, or it might have been called three drinks later, that a voice at his elbow spoke his name. He turned and saw Elaine standing there, Elaine whom he had last seen in the coffin, the wide blue eyes beneath the broad brow, the air not of innocence but of complete youthful candour, the shoulder-length fair hair, it was Elaine who had come back to him in an unfamiliar dress. That was what he thought for the moment in which he stared at her, spellbound. Then she spoke, and the spell was broken.

"I've got some scripts for you," the girl said in a childish, confident voice. "Mr Pannell thought you might not be coming back to the office, and asked if I would bring them over."

He took the papers and kept on staring. The girl was taller than Elaine and her figure was more coltish, less neat. The likeness was a matter of facial expression, that was all. "Just a zombie, massa boss," he said. "Only that and nothing more."

"What's that?"

"Nothing. What's your name?"

"Jennifer Masterson. I was – working late, and Mr Pannell asked me to bring over the papers."

"You're new, aren't you?"

"I've been in the office three weeks."

"First job, straight from finishing school?" She blushed. "Do you like it?"

"Oh, yes, it's terrific fun."

Fun, fun? It was so long ago that he had thought of anything as *fun* that the word had lost its meaning. "Miss Lake here doesn't think it's fun, and I'm not sure Mr Welcome does either." Her glance was awe-struck. These were gods, not to be treated flippantly. "Do you want to be a journalist?"

"Of course. On the paper – *The Plain Man*, I mean. I think Mr Gaye is wonderful, don't you? I mean, what he did for the Cameron family, and that's only one thing. Of course, some of the stuff in the paper goes too far, I think – those articles about the church I thought were horrible, really, although I'm not a churchgoing person myself. But I do think that really the editor should have – "

She stopped, appalled. Dex waved a hand. "Do go on, Miss Whatsit. What should the editor have done?"

Her face was scarlet. "I'm sorry."

"No need to apologise, we're all friends here. But I must go home. Back to dearest Marian, my everloving." Dex was quite visibly upset. He downed his drink, picked up hat and brief-case, put on his raincoat, waved, was gone.

"Oh, dear," the girl said. "I shouldn't have said that."

Nobody contradicted her. Francie and Bill Stead were engaged in some sort of wrangling conversation. Boy Kirton stared at the girl. He looked from face down to ringless hands.

"Look, Miss – Miss Masterson. Come out and have dinner with me. This evening."

"Oh," she said doubtfully. "I've got some more work to do. For Mr Pannell."

"I absolve you from it. I will tell Mr Pannell in the morning that I asked you to do some vitally urgent work for me."

"Do you think it will be all right?

"I don't think. I'm sure."

"I shall have to get my coat." She looked at him as though he might have disappeared by the time she came back.

"I shall be waiting. Impatiently."

She smiled at him, and the smile was Elaine's. When the door had swung to behind her Francie burst out laughing. "Oh, dear, Boy, I never expected to see you go in for baby farming. She reminds you of your dear departed, is that it?"

"Francie, you really are a bitch."

"I laugh so that I may not weep. Beneath this scaly exterior beats the most sensitive of hearts, so soft-boiled that it can never wield the executioner's axe." She leaned over until her face was close to his. "Haven't you ever wanted to get out of it, Boy, deep in your soft-boiled middle don't you want that?"

"I don't know."

"Speak for yourself, Francie." That was Bill Stead. "I find life not madly ethical perhaps, but very exciting. I mean to say, you never know where you are, do you, sacked one minute and back on the job the next."

"Storywise it's unethical, as Dex would say." She rocked with laughter. It seemed a miracle that she did not fall from the stool. "Take me home, Bill."

Bill Stead took her back in a taxi to the flat off Baker Street. He did not go in but waited while she turned the key in the lock, marvelling at the steadiness of her hand.

Boy Kirton took Jennifer Masterson out to dinner and talked about himself as he had not talked since Elaine died. As he talked and she listened the mists of actuality seemed to clear away and he saw not what he was but what he had imagined himself to be eight years ago, the bright young man to whom working for Ocky Gaye had been a kind of joke. Jennifer Masterson acted as unwitting accomplice to this piece of self-deception. She listened avidly to tales of the brilliantly ingenious stunts they had pulled off, the fakes they had exposed, the ways in which they had put the screws on cheating landlords and unscrupulous councils, the inauguration of the Traffic Protest Committee which had produced three perfectly good plans for curing traffic congestion providing the Government was prepared to spend a hundred million pounds a year, the campaign against Government boards controlling this and that, which had brought them support from industrialists all over the country. Jennifer Masterson listened and then talked herself, hesitantly at first, advancing ideas that he now knew to be ridiculously naïve, but doing so with an earnestness that charmed him. Her father, she said, was Sir John Masterson, and he had got her the job with *The Plain Man.* Kirton was surprised.

"I shouldn't have thought he'd have wanted – " He left the sentence unfinished.

"Daddy admires Mr Gaye very much. He's a banker, well not a banker, exactly, but something like that. On lots of boards." Masterson, Masterson? The name had some vague connotation for him, one of those complicated things about a finance house, something he didn't understand. "Daddy says *The Plain Man* seems to be muck-raking just for the sake of it rather too often, but he doesn't blame Mr Gaye for that. You know, he really is wonderful on television, isn't he, so sympathetic. And in the office, too, he always has a word for everybody. It was terrible, what I said in front of Mr Welcome, but really, I believe it's true. I think *The Plain Man* needs a new editor, somebody who's really sincere. Mr Gaye just can't realise the effect of some of the things that are printed in the paper."

He didn't mean to argue, but couldn't resist saying, "Are you sure those aren't the very things that make people read it?"

"I suppose so, in a way, but I believe just as many people would read it, more perhaps, if you cut out all the – well, the nastiness. I don't mean just sex."

They talked away for hours. Then he took her home to a narrow, elegant house just off Wilton Place, and left without even kissing her. "It's been a wonderful evening, Mr Kirton," she said. In the lamplight he saw Elaine's eyes looking at him.

Chapter Ten

It is part of the deep hypocrisy of the English that they condemn
nobody until they have been in prison, and that once they have
been sentenced, public reputation, as Oscar Wilde and Horatio
Bottomley found, is unsalvageable. Ocky Gaye had never been
in prison, never even been made bankrupt, and people still came
to his dinner parties. Not the most important people perhaps,
not members of the Cabinet, nor the very first rank of scientists,
nor the most famous military men, nor the most distinguished
dons, but Ocky's dinner-parties were still varied and curious.
On this particular October Tuesday, when Daniel Deacon was
confronting Joe Mycock in Colindale, and Francie Lake was
looking at his photograph in her flat, Ocky was welcoming a
collection of guests that included a retired Vice-Admiral who
had some theories about conducting the next war solely with
nuclear submarines, a French politician who had stepped off the
de Gaulle band-wagon and had formed a Small Peasants and
Freeholders Party, a much-married actress whose account of her
love affairs was being ghosted for *The Plain Man,* a film starlet
who was known to be the mistress of the Minister of
Propaganda, a Labour MP who had recently refused the party
whip on the ground that Labour foreign policy was now totally
reactionary, a solicitor associated with the formation of a new
amalgamated trust, a woman scientist who believed that the
problems involved in the development of nuclear energy could
be solved by the world-wide adoption of a vegetarian diet, and a

couple of television producers who prowled round this tasty meal of eccentrics like foxes after chickens.

It was part of Ocky's skill that he was able to mould such a job lot of oddities into a coherent group, so that the actress listened with apparent interest to the views of the Labour MP, the scientist expounded her views on nutrition to one of the television producers, and the retired Vice-Admiral demonstrated the certainty of mutual destruction to the solicitor. Ocky welded all of them with his unfailing good humour and his air of having in his time known everybody and done everything. All of Ocky's dinner-parties, as his wife Claire knew, had a purpose and she wondered, as she drank just a glass too much wine, what was the purpose of this one. A fund-raising enterprise? But there was nobody here, except perhaps the solicitor, who was likely to be useful in that way. What was the object of it, then? Here they were, drinking Ocky's wine and laughing at his jokes and listening as he spoke solemnly about Britain's future, but what did it mean more than that? A little woozily she asked him this when, just before midnight, the last of the guests had gone and they were alone in the ugly drawing-room furnished in no taste.

Ocky was hardly ever irritable, but his euphoria was notably diminished by the departure of their guests. The conversation of a company of people was like strong drink to him. So now he said simply that this sort of thing kept the wheels going round.

"What wheels?" Claire was plump and blonde, the daughter of a rich industrialist who had been given a peerage for his apparently inexhaustible flow of contributions to party funds. It is possible that Ocky had married her under the impression that part of this monetary river might be diverted to Plain Man Enterprises, but if so he was soon undeceived. The industrialist had made it clear from the start that Ocky was a son-in-law barely to be tolerated and certainly not to be encouraged or supported. Claire, however, remained utterly devoted to him, and she had developed over the years an intuitive sensibility that was sometimes alarming. Now she said, "Something's wrong, Ocky. What is it, the cash not coming in?"

"Nothing's wrong."

"I knew what you were like when we got married, or if I didn't I should have done. Everyone told me. I don't mind sitting round a table with crackpots like the ones who were here tonight, if it brings in the cash. That's all you want, isn't it?"

"Is that what you think? "He gripped her firm, beautiful shoulders. "You ought to know me better than that."

"I know you pretty well, at least I think so. What would you say if I told you I wanted a divorce?"

Startled, he let go of her, took a step back. "What for? You're not going with a man, are you?"

"Suppose I'm just tired of this sort of thing. Wouldn't you think that possible?"

"You're drunk."

"I dare say you're right." She put a hand to her forehead, then burst out laughing. "Oh, Ocky, you do look funny. What's yours belongs to you, and you'll never let it go, that's right, isn't it? Don't bother to contradict, I've seen it before. I don't believe you care two hoots about *The Plain Man* or anything, you just want to own people."

He grinned at her, good humour restored. "You've had too much to drink, ducks. Come to bed."

"Ocky, I'm serious."

"So am I."

"Not about a divorce, I don't mean that, but I know something's wrong. I can tell the signs. I just want to say I'm on your side, I don't care what you've done. Anything you want, the way it said in the film, you just have to whistle." She swayed slightly on her feet, a woman with a pearly attractiveness just short of beauty.

He began to laugh. "Come to bed."

As he led her upstairs she clung to him passionately, her body shaking. He patted her as he might have done a horse, made soothing noises, helped her to undress and put her to bed. Once in bed she turned blue eyes on him and said, "I love you, Ocky." The eyes were bright as signal lamps. Then eyelids closed, lamps went out. She was asleep.

Chapter Eleven

Bettridge pushed open the swing doors and Ocky, flower in buttonhole, bulky but wonderfully neat, walked into the hall of Plain Man Enterprises. Everybody began to smile and move, the commissionaires who were standing around, the Polish liftman who had been saved by Ocky from deportation, two or three idle girls. Ocky nodded, beamed, ducked his head left and right, brought them to life like a magician. He went up in his private lift, trotted along the corridor trailed by the cadaverous Bettridge, sat down at his big desk and began to dictate letters at a tremendous rate. Ocky called recording machines damned impersonal things, and always dictated to a secretary. When he had done with Bettridge he looked through the post and called in Mercury Ellis.

"What's on the plate this morning?"

"Ten o'clock Mr Welcome, he wants to talk to you about a possible racecourse doping series, half-past, Miss Spick – "

"Who's Miss Spick?"

"Head of some Council group in the Midlands, they say some of the councillors have been making a profit out of the sewers. I tried to put her on to Mr Welcome, but she said she must see you. Lunch, twelve-thirty, Mr O'Malley."

Peter O'Malley was one of Ocky's pipelines to the House of Commons, a journalist MP who sold scraps of information which were lively rather than accurate, and at times even ghosted articles which Ocky patched, stitched, and then signed with his name.

"That's all? Splendid. It's unfair you should have all those vital statistics and be efficient too."

She did not smile. For three months Ocky had been promising her more money. "I wanted to ask you – "

"About money. I know. This isn't the time. I am not in the giving mood. Do you know who said that?"

"No."

"Come and tell me when you've found out. Tell Ray Pillin I want to see him when he comes in. And Miss Lake. I don't want them together."

Mercury only just refrained from banging the door when she went out. Half a minute later her sulky voice said on the telephone, "Miss Lake doesn't answer. Mr Pillin's coming in."

Ray Pillin's air was conspiratorial. "Ran into a bit of trouble, Chief."

"You didn't get the pictures?"

"I got the pix all right, but – " He told the story of what had happened. Ocky listened, his squashy nose wrinkling in disgust.

"The way some people behave," he said perfectly seriously. "You simply can't trust them. Have you paid the other six?"

"Not yet."

"Get the money from cash, call it photographic expenses, add another five to it. Will that keep him happy?"

"I don't know about happy. He won't talk, if that's what you mean – as long as he isn't asked too many questions."

"He won't be asked any questions at all."

"All right, then. I took the pix and negs along to Francie, about half-ten it was."

"Did she say anything about them?"

"She didn't open them when I was there, just put them into a drawer of her dressing-table."

Dex poked his piggy head in at the door. Ocky asked him to wait, tried Francie's extension, got no reply, and asked Mercury to locate her. When Mercury rang back she sounded less bored than usual.

"She hasn't come in yet, and I'm getting an unobtainable ring from her number. I've had it checked, and they say the receiver must be off."

"That's queer."

"About that quotation – "

"Not now." Ocky was frowning as he spoke to Ray Pillin. "Francie's not come in yet, and her number's unobtainable. Go round there, will you. I don't want anything to go wrong with this."

When Ray Pillin had gone he let in Dex, who began to talk almost before he was inside the door. "I particularly wanted you to have a look at this material, because it really has got something new in it. There's this boy Lomax, who's been on the inside of half a dozen stables, and can give us chapter and verse. Promotion-wise there's no doubt it's a good story, if we can make the facts stick. Now my idea is this, a lot of tipsters are in on the story, know what happens. I've had their tips over three months collated with the material from Lomax and, factwise, it checks."

Dex always talked most when he was least certain.

Ocky sank back in his chair, looked at the photographs on the wall and at the Epstein head, listened and occasionally spoke. Dex was still talking when the telephone rang. It was Ray Pillin, and the little man was almost incoherent with excitement.

"Chief, Francie, she's here."

"Yes?"

"She's dead, Chief. She's been stabbed, murdered. At least, that's the way it looks."

"Have you told the police?"

"Not yet."

"You'd better do it, then. Where are you, in the flat?"

"No, in a call-box. The telephone in the flat is lying on the floor, off the hook, thought I'd better not touch it. But, Chief, this is the thing. The pix aren't here."

"Oh. Is there much of a mess? I mean, has somebody searched for them?"

"I'll say there's a mess, stuff all over the place. But Chief – Chief – "

"Yes?"

"When I ring the police they're going to tell me to stay here, then ask me questions. What am I going to say?"

Ocky put his hand over the receiver and nodded dismissively. When Dex had gone, bearing himself with an air of conscious martyrdom, the little man spoke to Ray Pillin and told him what to say.

Chapter Twelve

The body lay on the living-room floor, near a bookcase. There was a trail of blood from the middle of the room across to the bookcase, and it seemed that for some reason she had crawled across the floor. To reach the telephone, perhaps? She had pulled out one of the books from the case and it lay beside her on the floor. She, had also, presumably, pulled down the telephone, but died before she was able to use it.

She lay almost on her back. There was a good deal of blood on the pink night-dress she wore and it was possible by bending down, as Superintendent Nevers did, to see that there were at least two stab wounds in her chest. She had been wearing bedroom slippers, one of which had fallen off. Apart from the stab wounds there were, as far as Nevers could tell from a cursory examination, no other marks of violence.

What had happened? The woman had gone to bed – the bed had been occupied – and had been roused by a visitor. Apparently she knew this visitor. At least she had not troubled to put on a dressing-gown or to remove the night cream from her face. Did he possess a key, or had he rung the bell? If he had rung, it might be possible to check the time. (Nevers reminded himself that the gender was used only for the sake of convenience.) Had they talked, argued? There was no sign that they had either drunk or smoked. In one corner of the sitting-room was a typewriter on a small table, and in the typewriter was an unfinished letter. It provided one of the puzzles in the case.

Either the visitor had let himself in with a key, or the woman had come out and opened the door. He had evidently come for some purpose other than murder, although that might have been in his mind too. Had he asked her for something which she refused to give him? The room was in a mess – a lamp standard overturned, underclothes taken out of the chest of drawers and left on the floor, photographs and letters lying around. He had either got what he came for or given up the search and left. Presumably he had taken the murder weapon with him. At least, there was no sign of it in the flat. He had left her for dead, but she had not been quite dead. She had crawled over towards the bookcase, pulled down the telephone, which was on a small table beside it, died before she could dial for the police. At the same time, apparently, she had deliberately pulled from the bookcase the book that lay under her hand, a book called – Nevers bent sideways to look at the title – *Great Victorian Journalists* by J. Catchment. Her actions didn't seem quite to fit together. And the unfinished letter, that didn't fit in at all.

The letter was just being extracted from the typewriter. Sergeant Quick stood directing the fingerprint men, who dealt with it as gingerly as though it were some fragment of the Dead Sea Scrolls. Nevers went over, and the two of them stood looking down at the sheet of ordinary copy paper. The letter read:

1.45 a.m. Tuesday night or rather
Wednesday morning

Dear Ocky,

I've decided that I just can't go on any more. I can't take it. Will you please accept this letter as my resignation, as of now.

I don't imagine you'll want reasons. You know well enough that you've changed over the years, that the paper isn't anything like what it was when we set out, a long time ago now and it seems much longer, on some sort of crusade. You'll say I've changed too. I dare say. But that doesn't make it any better. Perhaps it's not too late to make something out of my life. Anyway, I want out.

No tears, for the past, no foolishness. Nowadays the sky looks grey every morning, then it seemed a permanent blue. That's all nonsense. But the past crowds in all the time. I've been looking at old photographs, but I don't need them to remind me. Remember that antique Austin we used on that trip to Wales when the paper was three months old, and the way you swore when the chap in Swansea drove into us and bent the fender? Yes, the past comes crowding in all right if you let it, but I'm going to think about the future. I'll let you into a secret, Ocky.

Here, rather more than half-way down the page, the typescript ended.

"Queer, sir, isn't it?" Quick said.

Nevers agreed. Nothing about the letter fitted. On the face of it the woman had sat down at her typewriter at a quarter to two in the morning, and begun to type this letter. She had given it up, and gone to bed without removing it from the machine. This seemed unlikely. It was much more probable that the murderer had typed the letter himself. But with what object – to fake a time for the murder?

"Do you think it's a plant?" The sergeant echoed his thoughts.

"If there are prints on that piece of paper – "

One of the fingerprint men came up. "Nothing on that sheet but a couple of smudges at one edge, sir. Can't make anything of them. There are some prints on the machine."

Nevers nodded, made a face. The smudges could have been made deliberately by the murderer to avoid a fingerprint, or they could be accidental. The prints on the typewriter would probably be those of the dead woman.

"She might have started to type a draft of a letter of resignation which she was going to write out in longhand afterwards, then given up and gone to bed so that she could think it over in the morning," Quick said. Nevers gave an unencouraging grunt. "You know who Ocky is, it's that chap Gaye, the Plain Man."

"Yes, I've grasped that. And her name's Lake."

"That's right, sir, Frances Lake. The chap who's waiting outside, little man named Pillin, the one who found her, works for Gaye too. Seems very much on edge, a bit more than you'd expect."

"I'll talk to him in a minute. Hallo, Doctor."

Doctor Lawry was a tall lean grizzled man, and he showed little interest in the body on the floor." Haven't got much time. How soon will your men be through?"

"Five minutes." Nevers spoke again to Quick. "Those photographs and letters on the floor, collect 'em up and take a look through them. I don't suppose there's anything – whether or not he found what he was looking for, he won't have left anything compromising on the floor – but you never know. We'll have to go through them in detail later on. All right for Doctor Lawry, boys? He's in a hurry."

"As always," one of the photographers said.

Lawry was humorous. "I can tell you she won't want much lunch today." He knelt down by the body.

Nevers went out to talk to Pillin. He saw a small rat-faced man with peering eyes, yellow teeth, and an air of conspicuous nervousness. They talked in the tiny passage that led along to the bedroom and kitchen from the entrance door.

"Just tell me, Pillin, why you came along here this morning?"

"It was to get some pix – pictures – back from Miss Lake, pictures I'd left here last night for her to look at."

"What sort of pictures?"

"We'd been thinking of running a series in the paper, that's *The Plain Man, I* expect you know it, about Army brutality, the sort of thing boys have to go through when they join up, and I'd been developing the pix. I brought them round here to Miss Lake last night, so that she could look at them."

"Did you take these pictures yourself?"

"Oh, no. I just developed the negs."

"Where did they come from?"

"You'd have to ask Mr Gaye that."

Pillin's manner, a blend of slyness and obsequiousness, irritated Nevers. A recollection stirred in his mind. "Pillin your name is, you said. Don't I know you?"

The little man scuffed his shoes together. "I don't think so."

"Indecent photographs, right? You were lucky to get away with a fine."

Shyly, looking down at his feet, Pillin murmured, "I've been unfortunate."

"Those photographs you're talking about, they weren't that kind of thing?"

"Oh, no, sir. They were just, you know, boys marching with full kit and being made to stand against a wall with their hands above their heads, all that sort of thing. We thought it might make a feature."

"Why should Miss Lake want to see these pictures? What were they to do with her?"

"She's the general manager of the whole group. Mr Gaye relies on her a lot."

"What time last night did you bring round the pictures?"

"About half ten."

"Half-past ten," Nevers said pedantically. "Was she fully dressed?"

"Yes, she was, that's right."

"Did you notice anything odd about her manner? Anything at all that struck you as strange?"

"She'd had a few drinks, but that was nothing. She could carry her liquor, Francie." Unexpectedly and absurdly, Pillin dabbed at his eyes with a dirty handkerchief.

"Did she say anything that indicated she might be expecting somebody?"

"No. But I wasn't here more than a couple of minutes, just handed over the pix and went."

"Did she look at them while you were here?"

Pillin hesitated for a moment before saying, "No." Nevers' doubt that he was being told a true story increased. His tone sharpened.

"What brought you here this morning?" Pillin explained the course of events in the office that had led to his visit. "Why were the photographs wanted urgently?"

Again Pillin said, "You'd have to ask Mr Gaye."

"I will. Now, you came here, rang the bell – "

"That's right. And no reply. Then I pushed the door and it was open, see. So I came into the passage here and called Francie's name. She didn't answer, so I looked in there." His widespread hands suggested the rest.

"Did you touch anything in the room?"

"Well, I'd come to collect the pix. But they weren't here. At least I couldn't see them."

"You mean you touched those photographs and letters lying around?"

Pillin's shoes scuffed together. "Some of them. I didn't think – "

"You're right you didn't. Did you find the pictures you brought last night?"

"No."

"They've been taken?"

"Francie may have passed 'em on to someone. I didn't find them, that's all."

"You won't object to being searched." Pillin, protesting feebly, was searched. No pictures of any kind were found on him. Nevers asked a few more questions, then let him go. He told Quick about the interview.

"You don't think he was telling the truth, sir?"

"Put it this way, lies come naturally to him. I wouldn't trust him farther than I could throw him."

"It will be interesting to see whether Gaye confirms his story, though I suppose he may have rung Gaye before he spoke to us."

"Ten to one on, if you ask me. Gaye's a champion liar, and whatever it is he's been mixed up in you can bet it's crooked."

"Oh, I don't know, sir. He's done a lot of good work." Sergeant Quick was a furtive admirer of *The Plain Man.* "Did you see that TV programme two or three weeks ago when – "

"He was campaigning for all police pay to be doubled. I think we've all heard about that. Do you think he believes a word of what he says?"

Quick grinned. "I don't much care whether he believes it, sir, as long as he says it. I could do with a bit more in my pay packet."

"You won't get it through Ocky Gaye. Where's Lawry – has he finished yet?"

"Here he is." The doctor spoke from behind them. "The woman's dead, I can confirm it. She was stabbed twice with a long, thin, narrow blade, I couldn't identify it more exactly than that for you. Something like a flick knife, but longer. She died within minutes, and by that I mean probably within five minutes."

"Would she have been able to crawl a yard or two across the room, so that she could pull down the telephone and that book before she died?"

"I wouldn't have thought so, quite honestly. But there's a blood trail leading that way, so it looks as though I must be wrong." Lawry beamed.

"If she died within five minutes of being stabbed, the murderer must have left the flat almost immediately, because obviously he'd never have left her alone to crawl over to the telephone." Lawry made no comment. "What about time of death?"

"You always ask the most difficult questions. Let's say – oh, between midnight and three ack emma, shall we?"

"You can't get any nearer?"

"If you want my personal opinion now, I'd say it was between one and two in the morning. But professional caution, you know, allow an hour either side. Oh, by the way, no sexual interference, just a good honest stabbing job." He put a finger to his nose, winked at them, and left.

"What's he got to be so cheerful about?" Quick said, looking after the doctor's jaunty retreating figure.

"They love to set us puzzles. Now look, Quick, there seem to be two lines of approach at the moment. Either she was killed as a result of her activities on behalf of *The Plain Man,* and goodness knows they must often have given reason for murder, or through something connected with her private life, perhaps the surprise mentioned in that letter."

"If the letter's genuine."

"Even if the letter's a fake there may really be a secret. We'll work on these two lines."

"You want me to go and see Gaye?" Quick was a little too eager.

"You'd be down on your knees in a couple of minutes, asking him to let you say thank you for the wonderful work he's doing for the police. No, my boy. I'll tackle Gaye, for the time being at least. You stay here, talk to the neighbours – you'll find enough of them gawping round outside – and people in the other flats. If they heard anything, saw anybody, so much the better. Put a couple of men on to that. And I want you to try to find out what sort of a woman she was, what people thought of her, did she have men friends, what they looked like. Got it?"

"Got it."

"And I want the case history of that little Pillin. Let me have his record, and notes on what he's doing now."

"Anything else?"

If there was any irony in Quick's voice, Nevers apparently did not perceive it. "Not at the moment."

Chapter Thirteen

Superintendent Nevers was unimaginative but shrewd, a man with a great feeling for tradition, authority, and what he would have called the decencies of life. He had an inherent dislike of demagogues and of people who wanted to change things, and he was hostile to almost all of the things he believed Ocky Gaye to represent. He was not, therefore, disposed to be impressed by the big office, the big desk, the expanse of carpet. He did not recognise the bronze head as being by Epstein, but he regarded it as showing off to display this piece of sculpture in such close proximity to the original. He had been contemptuously prepared for the necessity of walking over that big stretch of carpet while the tin-pot dictator at the desk sat waiting for him. But the tin-pot dictator did nothing of the kind. He was up, out of his chair and round the desk, hastening over the carpet before Nevers had taken half a dozen steps inside the room. His handshake was warm and firm, the large blue-grey eyes were serious, the beautiful voice clear but hushed, on a cathedral note.

"Sit down, Mr Nevers. This is a terrible thing. You'll want to talk to me, of course."

"Yes."

"And to question members of my organisation, no doubt."

"That too."

"I'm absolutely at your service." To the blonde secretary who stood poised rather consciously beside the desk he said,

Mercury, tell Mr O'Malley I can't meet him for lunch. Explain what's happened. Ask if he can have a word with me later today. Will you want me after lunch?"

"I shouldn't think so."

"You'd better cancel all my appointments until three-thirty, Mercury. Now, Superintendent, you won't take a drink on duty, but will you smoke a cigarette? No. Then I'll start talking. Would you like me to do that, or would you sooner ask me questions?"

"It will suit me if you tell me what you know about this affair. I can ask questions later."

Ocky got up and paced the room on his little legs, pausing occasionally to look out of the big window or to glance at the John portrait. "I think I ought to tell you about Francie. Come here, Mr Nevers – can I drop the Superintendent? Look at this photograph."

Nevers looked at the photograph which showed her with Ocky, Ocky holding in his hand the first issue of *The Plain Man*. "That was taken twelve years ago. You'd hardly know her as the same woman. You saw her this morning?"

"Yes." Matter of factly, Nevers said, "Of course, she'd been stabbed."

"If you're going to understand Francie, and my own guess would be that the key to her murder rests in the sort of person she was, you've got to understand the change in her. You've got to understand what caused the change. I did." Nevers said nothing. "The girl in that picture was young, gay, idealistic. She believed England could be changed for the better, and she thought I was the person to do it. The woman who died didn't believe any of those things. She was disappointed in me, and that meant she was disappointed in the world."

"This is a copy of a letter that was found in the typewriter in her room."

Ocky read it, his face impassive. "May I keep it?"

"All right." Sharply Nevers said, "Don't you want to say anything about it?"

"What is there to say?"

"You had no idea she was intending to leave you?"

"She made no bones about being dissatisfied. But as for leaving – no, I had no idea."

"You don't know what she means by telling you a secret?" Ocky shook his head. "But you think the letter's genuine?"

"Don't you?"

Nevers was cautious. "I just have it in mind that it *could* have been written by somebody else who knew the circumstances of her life. That's so, isn't it?"

"I suppose so, yes."

"What I don't understand is this." Nevers leaned forward. "If she was that much dissatisfied why didn't she leave you, do something else?"

"You don't give up the habits of a lifetime like that. At least Francie didn't. We had an affair years ago. It was all over, but emotionally Francie was stuck with me. She didn't like what was happening here, but she couldn't get away." Ocky smiled. "You don't like *The Plain Man* much yourself, do you?"

Nevers felt himself being trapped into a personal relationship. He found that he positively wanted to tell the little man why he disliked *The Plain Man* and what it stood for. Instead he said stolidly, "That's neither here nor there."

"You're right. I'm drawing a picture, you understand that, don't you? You may have found letters from me in her flat. I don't know, but it's very likely you have. They refer to two different people, people who don't exist any more. Bear that in mind when you read them. I kept Francie here because she was a damned good administrator, that's what she'd turned into poor girl. She was the general manager of the whole group."

"Was she liked?"

"Liked," Ocky repeated in surprise. He grinned. "It isn't the job of a general manager to be liked, nobody does that sort of work well and gets liked for it."

Ploddingly Nevers asked, "Might that be a reason for her murder?"

"I suppose it's possible. She was pretty rough and tough, as anybody in that job has to be. She was the only one here I really trusted and the editorial boys all knew that, but no, I shouldn't say it was the reason why she was killed."

Still with his plodding stiff solidity Nevers said, "Then it doesn't concern me much, does it?"

"God damn it." Ocky stopped pacing and stared at him. "What do you want? I'm trying to make a picture for you, show you what she was like, and you say it's no help and you don't want it. Do you think I've got no feelings, do you think I like telling you all this? But if you're not interested I'll shut up. You go ahead and ask questions. I'll just answer them." He pressed the button on his desk and the cocktail cabinet moved out. Ocky poured himself a drink.

Nevers was obscurely conscious of confusion, of boorishness. "Do you mind if I change my mind and have one, after all."

The smile that irradiated Ocky's face was charming. "Whisky?"

"Thanks."

"Nice of you. I don't like drinking alone."

In some way, and against Nevers' intentions, sympathy had been established. Am I doing that much better than Quick? the superintendent wryly wondered, as he asked Ocky to go on talking.

"I'd nearly come to the end of this background stuff. We were still pretty close in a curious way, Francie and I, but it's possible that she had some relationship with a member of the staff that I don't know about. But my guess would be that her murder was linked with something not connected with the office at all, but mixed up with her private life. She lived a rackety life in an odd way, picked up men in night clubs, took them home with her. I only know about it because sometimes, when she was feeling really nasty, she used to tell me. In a way it reflected on me, if you see what I mean."

"You don't know of any particular man?"

"No. I should say it was likely she got mixed up with somebody who took her seriously, and killed her when he found out she wasn't serious, too."

"There's another possibility," Nevers said dryly. "Your man Pillin's been in touch with you, no doubt. He's told you that the photographs he left with Miss Lake are missing."

"Yes, he's told me. I don't really understand why anybody should take them."

"Tell me what they were, will you, how many of them and so on. In detail. The whole story. Just as you did about Miss Lake," he added with a touch of sarcasm.

Before Ocky could begin again there was a tap on the door. A girl wearing a waitress' uniform wheeled in a trolley containing a large turkey, a ham, an ox tongue, and a variety of salads. On the lower shelf were fresh strawberries, peaches, apricots. There was a bottle in a bucket that rattled with ice. The trolley was followed by a man in a white coat and a chef's hat, who brandished a carving knife and fork.

"Do forgive me," Ocky said. "I foresaw that my – interrogation, shall I call it? – would extend over the lunch hour. You won't refuse a slice of turkey and a glass of wine?"

"I – "

"I assure you that it won't delay things. Once the bird is carved I'll talk between mouthfuls. And after all, you have to eat lunch somewhere."

Ocky was grinning. Nevers felt that it would be impossibly churlish to refuse. Why should he refuse, anyway? And yet, as he ate the turkey and ham and drank the wine, which hadn't quite enough body for his taste, he felt that somehow Ocky had got the better of him. The little man was as good as his word. While he ate he talked.

"We get all kinds of stuff brought in to us here, and whatever you may think, we're careful about what we use. This story came from a soldier named Patterson who said that in his unit, I can't tell you the exact unit offhand, but it's in our records, in his unit recruits were being frog-marched, made to drill at the double in full marching kit, made to stand up against the wall in one position for three hours at a time, and so forth. Real Nazi stuff. Patterson was told that his story was no good unless he could produce photographs. He had a chum in the unit who used to be a photographer. He took some pictures and smuggled them out. You realise it was a risky business to do that, if they'd been caught those two boys would have been for the high jump. They smuggled out negatives. I got Ray Pillin to develop them, and take them round to Francie."

"Why not to you?"

"I had a dinner party last night, too busy to look at them. Besides, I trusted Francie's judgement over things like that."

"What was the hurry?"

"That shows you don't know much about the magazine world. There's always a hurry." Ocky looked at the turkey leg he had been gnawing, put it on the side of his plate, wiped greasy fingers and face with a napkin. "Patterson and his friend are in a hurry to get paid, we're in a hurry to print the story if it's genuine. There's always a hurry."

"Why did the pictures go to her and not to the editor of *The Plain Man*? I should have thought that would be the natural thing."

Ocky belched. "You might think so, it might even be true in an ordinary set-up, but here you'd be wrong. Dex Welcome, that's the editor you're talking about, isn't even a yes man, he's a don't know man. He's a good editor in other ways, but he'd like a committee to make up his mind for him. You like committees?"

"Not particularly."

"I don't. We've got no committees here. Either I make up Dex's mind or Francie does. Sometimes when I'm in a bad mood I make Dex do it for himself. That really upsets him." He grinned. "I wasn't available so the pictures went to Francie, right?"

"I suppose so." But Nevers had the feeling that it wasn't right, although he could not have said why. "Then this morning you wanted to see the pictures, so you sent Pillin round for them. Was it that urgent?"

"Have some fruit." While Nevers ate delicate strawberries Ocky went on talking. "Francie was like me, always here early in the morning. When she wasn't in by ten o'clock I knew something had happened. Couldn't get her on the phone, so I sent Ray round."

"Why do you employ Pillin?"

"He's a good photographer, so I'm told."

"He's got a record."

"He's got a record," Ocky mimicked him. He leaned back and roared with laughter. Nevers flushed slightly. "Do you think I care whether he's got a record or not, as long as he suits me. I know what you think about me, you're thinking I'm lucky not to have a record myself. I won't say whether I think you're right or not. But you can see I might have a fellow feeling for Ray Pillin now, can't you?"

Nevers found it more difficult than Ocky to talk while eating. His next words came out slightly strangled. "Do you know of any reason, any reason at all, why those photographs should have been stolen?"

"As a blind." Nevers stared in surprise. "Look at it this way. Who knew those pictures were going to be in Francie's flat last night? Just the three of us, Ray, Francie and I. What would be the point of my stealing them? And why should Ray bother to steal them when he could easily make extra copies if he wanted to cheat on me? The only people who could conceivably have wanted to steal them are the officers and n.c.o.s in the pictures, but there's no way they could have known they were in Francie's flat. What can it have been but a blind, then? The chap who killed Francie saw these photographs, took them to mix things up. This was a killing with some personal motive in it, believe me."

When Nevers left Ocky's presence ten minutes later he felt as though he had been exposed to a powerful attempt to control his personality, made by a hypnotist. What was worse, he was not at all certain, in spite of his brave assertion of individuality, that he had not in fact been hypnotised.

Chapter Fourteen

When Nevers had gone Ocky sat staring straight in front of him for a little while. It might have appeared that he was looking at the John portrait, but in fact, he did not see it. He was making a rapid calculation of risks and possibilities, ways and means. A boy came in with the noon editions of the evening papers, and he glanced at them. They contained the story, with a headline, but it was no more than a paragraph. "Francie Lake, dynamic, glamorous top executive of Plain Man Enterprises, and rumoured to be the brains behind Ocky Gaye's empire, was found stabbed to death in her flat this morning – " one story began. Ocky snorted, and read no more. He rang for Mercury Ellis.

"Get me Dan Deacon. And when I'm through with him I want to talk to Boy Kirton."

"Richard the Third," she said.

"What?"

"That quotation. Richard the Third said it to Buckingham. But it's not mood, it's vein."

Ocky said with genuine admiration, "You're a smart girl. You're ignorant, Mercury, but you're smart." Squinting horribly, and raising one shoulder higher than the other, he got off his chair and rounded the desk, declaiming:

But I, that am not shaped for sportive tricks,
Nor made to court an amorous looking glass;

85

I, that am curtailed of this fair proportion,
Cheated of feature by dissembling nature,
Deformed, unfinished, sent before my time
Into this – something world.

He made a sudden grab at her. Mercury evaded him. "We were talking about money," she said, "when you told me to find out about the quotation. You said I was to come back and tell you."

"So you've told me."

"I'm still talking about money."

"Women, women." Ocky drew out his wallet and extracted a five-pound note. "Go out and buy yourself a new dress."

She made a disgusted face. "I thought it would be that much each week."

"You don't want it?" He put a plump hand over the note.

"Yes." He lifted his hand, put it down again as she reached for the note. "Say thank you."

"Thank you." She snatched the note and added, "For nothing."

Ocky caught hold of her, clasped her tightly to him, planted a fierce kiss on her lips. She broke free and slapped his face.

"I shouldn't do that again. I might tell my young man. He's a boxer."

He burst out laughing, laughed until the tears ran out of his eyes and drew out another note. "You said you wanted one every week. Here's next week's."

"And what about the one after that?"

"Come and see me when the time comes. Do you know who gave me this wallet? The Shoreditch Working Men's Club. For services to world peace." He started laughing again. There were times when Mercury wondered whether he was completely sane. She took the notes and left the room.

Ocky was squinting again, and muttering lines from *Richard The Third* when he heard Deacon's voice. Deacon had called in Miss Brocklebank.

"It's that man Gaye." Miss Brocklebank, who had been accustomed to hear Ocky's name mentioned in a different tone, hid her surprise. "I want you to listen on the line. Take down what's said and make a transcript afterwards. Do you understand?"

She nodded, mesmerised by his gravity. When Ocky said, "Dan, how are you?" she wrote it down in shorthand.

"We've got nothing to talk about."

"I just want to say this, Dan. I've thought over that proposition you made the other day. I'm afraid I flew off the handle. Can we talk about it again?"

Whatever Deacon had expected, it was not this. "You mean on my terms?"

"I was a little hasty." Ocky had no objection to using clichés when they provided an easy means of communication.

"Let's have this straight, Gaye. We should be talking on terms which would involve my financial and editorial control."

"I know, I know."

"Otherwise there would be no point in talking at all."

"I fully agree, Dan."

Deacon's instincts warned him to have nothing to do with Ocky. He hesitated.

"Would it be possible for me to stay on in some capacity?" Ocky's voice was humble. "That would be valuable for me. Couldn't we at least discuss that side of it?"

The scent of complete victory was strong. "You mean privately?"

"That's right, no lawyers, no accountants. Let's come to a personal agreement."

"On the terms I've outlined."

"Of course. Could you spare an hour today?"

"Just a minute." He buzzed Miss Brocklebank. "I haven't got anything important on this afternoon, have I? Good. I shall be talking to Mr Gaye. And Miss Brocklebank, don't bother about that transcript." He smiled. She retired, dazzled. Deacon arranged to see Ocky in his St. John's Wood house in an hour's time.

Deacon put down the receiver with a sigh of satisfaction. He saw, quite distinctly, a picture of himself as the head of a magazine empire, small at first although not insignificant, and enlarging rapidly with the years. He saw *The Plain Man,* stripped of its undesirable features, converted into a medium for the expression of his views about the world. He had forgotten all about Joe Mycock.

Deacon would have been astonished to see Ocky Gaye, after he had put down the telephone, bowing elaborately to the Epstein head, and then putting out his tongue at himself in a looking-glass. He began to hum, and did not stop when Mercury asked if he could see Ray Pillin.

The photographer was in a sad state of nerves. Ocky contemplated him with some distaste. "I told that copper the story you gave me, about the Army pix and that, but what was the good of it?"

"How do you mean?"

"The police will get on to this Army lark and they'll find out that the story's a phoney."

"It's not a phoney. You must trust your uncle Ocky a little more, my boy. Those Army pictures were taken, just as I said. When the police get on to the boys who took them they'll confirm everything I've said. Our only infraction of the truth was in saying that you delivered them to Francie."

"You're a wonder, Chief. But who do you think took our pix?"

"That's a problem I'm trying to solve. You just sit back and say nothing." Pillin began to whine something unintelligible. Ocky said unpleasantly, "You don't have any choice, really, do you? You're an accessory after the fact in a case of murder. And in case you should be thinking I'm an accessory too, I've only told that superintendent what you've told me. Keep your mouth shut, or you'll be slapped down so hard you'll never know what hit you."

Almost reproachfully, Ray Pillin said, "You don't have to talk to me like that, Chief."

"I know I don't. Trust in God and Uncle Ocky, and you'll be all right." The photographer was at the door when Ocky said, "I think this belongs to you." When Pillin looked at the bit of paper that had been pushed into his hand he found it was a note to the cash desk to pay him a hundred pounds.

Ocky pushed down the switch for Mercury and bellowed, "Where's Boy Kirton?" The door opened. "All right, he's here."

"It's terrible about Francie," Kirton said.

"Terrible, terrible. And it puts us on the spot, you understand that. This is just a beginning, the nationals are going to have a field day. This is a hell of a thing to have happened to me."

"It wasn't too nice for Francie, either."

Ocky glared. "Let's take it as read, shall we, that we're all sorry about Francie. But she's dead and we're alive. Have you thought about the effect this is going to have on the paper?"

"No." He had spent most of the morning thinking about Jennifer Masterson.

"Well, think about it if you want to stay in a job. This is a crisis. Francie's gone, we can't bring her back. We can find her murderer."

"Aren't the police doing that?"

"They're fussing about some missing pictures for an Army series. Nobody could possibly want them, it's a blind. I told the copper that, but he was too stupid to believe me. What I want you to do, Boy, is to start an investigation through *Crime Today*. Find out about Francie's life, what she did, who her boyfriends were. Brief what's his name, Smedley, on it, get him to work too, and anyone else you can spare."

"There are only five of us on the paper. We're not competent to do this sort of thing, you know it as well as I do."

Ocky had been walking up and down. Now he stopped. "What's the matter with you today?"

"The idea's a fake. It won't lead anywhere."

"That's what you think. We can make something of this, Boy, we can make a lot of it. I use it in the programme, show you and Smedley working on the investigation, start a real national campaign. If the police turn up the villain, well and good. If not we're helping them, don't you see it?"

He saw it, but he could not feel enthusiastic as he might have done a year, even a month, ago. He was at the door when Ocky called him back. The little man had a piece of paper in his hand.

"Take a look at this. It's a copy of a letter they found in the flat, in Francie's typewriter. The super let me see it."

He read it. "Unfinished. That means – "

"They think it means Francie was interrupted while she was typing. But to me it's got a smell about it. Can you smell the same thing, Boy?"

Something about the letter puzzled Kirton. "If she'd been going to say this sort of thing to you, she'd have written it in longhand."

"That's very true."

"It's rather like a clue in a detective story."

"Just the thought I was trying to put my finger on," Ocky said admiringly. "Anyway, I've had Mercury make some copies. You keep that one, see what you make of it."

Chapter Fifteen

Daniel Deacon was not a malicious man, but he felt a relish in the prospect of Ocky's discomfiture. The course of their negotiations had not been quite as Ocky, in whom the habit of misrepresentation was deeply ingrained, had told his friends. They had known each other for a long time, certainly, had sat on the same committees, although it was a long time now since Ocky had been invited to sit on any important committee. He and Bella had been guests at more than one of Ocky's dinner-parties, and he had admired the adroitness with which the little man used his guests for his own ends. There had been little luncheon parties, too, parties of half a dozen men, important men most of them, who had been enthusiastic about Ocky and his mission. Men like Sir Gravely Wilson, Lord Borboring, Hammond Hallett, Wiley Morecambe, Sir James Jeavons, names that meant something in engineering and steel and cotton, had come to the luncheon parties and had talked to and of Ocky as a man to be followed, a possible national saviour.

But in the last – how long? – the last two years, and certainly in the last year, since Jeavons' death, things had changed. There were different people, much less important people, at the little luncheon parties, and then there were no parties at all because, Ocky said, he hadn't time for them. Gravely Wilson had warned Deacon one day in the club that Ocky was a man best left alone, and the warning carried no less conviction because it was conveyed with Wilson's characteristic obliquity, the words left

91

unsaid being even more potent than those actually uttered. But to Deacon this warning had acted as an incentive. He smelt the decay of Ocky's empire, and saw the chance of fulfilling his ambition of becoming a press magnate, even though a small one. He had been prepared to wait, confident that one day he would be able to take over Plain Man Enterprises on his own terms. It was Ocky who had approached him with the suggestion that he should buy into the organisation and not the other way round, and Deacon had taken this as the signal for action. He had made it clear that he would want financial control, and Ocky had been agreeable but vague about this, implying that they could leave all such wretchedly bothersome details to the lawyers and accountants. Deacon's accountants had reported most unfavourably on the condition of Plain Man Enterprises, although Ocky's habitual confusion had made it difficult for them to discover the exact situation. Mr Trubly, of Trubly, Myers and Piggott, had complained that Mr Gaye couldn't be got to discuss affairs in proper detail. It was possible, and indeed it was to be hoped, that they were better than they looked. Mr Gaye, Trubly had added, was a charming man but not reliable. He was particularly unreliable, Trubly thought, on the editorial side, and he mentioned some of the recent payments made by Plain Man Enterprises to avoid libel actions. The size of these payments had come as a shock to Deacon, and it was after receiving Trubly's report that he had decided that he must have not only financial but editorial control. His breaking off of negotiations had been a strategic move, designed to bring Ocky to heel.

He was slightly annoyed to see Ocky driven up in his Rolls, and Levitt hastening to open the door, and holding an umbrella over the little man so that he should not be dampened between car and front door. It seemed the wrong car, and the wrong sort of entry, for a suppliant. Then Ocky was in the room and beaming at him, and asking for Bella.

"She's out on her good works. One of her Refugee Committees. She'll be sorry to have missed you." This was perfectly true, for Bella had a soft spot for Ocky who was, she had once said, such a little rogue that you couldn't help liking him.

"The most delightful woman I know." Ocky kissed the tips of his fingers. "You've seen this?"

It was a copy of the paper, with news of Francie Lake's murder. "No."

"She was my right hand."

"I don't think I'd met her."

"Ah, come on, Dan." Ocky plumped himself down in an armchair and crossed his little legs. Deacon stiffened. There was an unmistakable air of insolence in the way the words were spoken. He replied sharply.

"That's got nothing to do with what we were talking about on the telephone."

"Oh, yes, it has." Looking up at the grey, handsome figure who towered above him, Ocky said whimsically, "Where were you last night, Dan?"

The recollection of that curious interview in the suburban house came back to Deacon at once. More sharply, he said, "So it was blackmail. I should have thought you could have done better."

"Where were you between – oh, seven and eight o'clock, say? It's what they call a rhetorical question. I had you followed. I can tell you where you were. In a rather shady little hotel."

"You must be mad."

"You tell me then, Dan, you tell me where you were."

"Out in Colindale, talking to an agent of yours named Mycock. He tried to blackmail me. It was a stupid thing to do. I credited you with more sense, Gaye." Deacon bit off the words in the way that had terrified many a conference of executives, but he did not say *Get out*. He guessed, feared, that there was more to come, and he stood on his toes like a boxer, ready to ride the punch.

"Won't do, I'm afraid." Ocky was shaking his head, smiling sadly. "Prove it."

"What?"

"Prove you were there. Did you tell your secretary that was where you were going? Of course you didn't. Did you take your car out to Colindale? Not you."

"Mycock – " Deacon said and stopped.

"What will you bet that Mycock says he never saw you in his life? Don't bank on Mycock. You'd lose your money."

"What are you getting at?"

"I'm getting at where you really were, Dan. Better sit down." Deacon had no idea of what was coming, but he knew it would be bad. He sat down. "Just before seven o'clock you drove up with a young girl, a *very* young girl, to a hotel near Paddington. There's no need for me to name it. You gave the taxi-driver a handsome tip, just as well because from the look of the girl you'd been enjoying yourself in the taxi. You signed the book in the name of Mr and Mrs Dai Davies from Cardiff. Ah, yes, I forgot to say you didn't sign it yourself, you asked the clerk to do it. You went up to your room. And after that, as you very well know, Dan, your passions got the better of you. I won't go into details, but it wasn't nice. The girl screamed, the manager came up, threatened to call the police. You bribed your way out of it. Fortunately – well, *un*fortunately for you, I suppose I have to say – my chap who was following you took some photographs. They were interesting photographs, they showed you going in the hotel, and in the bedroom with the girl."

Deacon looked down at his hands. They were trembling. He put one hand on his knee. He said nothing.

"It's not just a matter of the photographs, you see," Ocky said mildly. "We've got statements from the manager and the desk clerk, they'll identify you, and very likely the taxi-driver will too. We can get a statement from the girl, and whether you knew it or not, she's under age. What have you got to put against that? Just this ridiculous tale of being down in Colindale. Then there's another thing. All this has happened before. There was that girl down in Wales, Gwyneth what's her name, after her association with you she was taken to an asylum, right? And you pay for her to be kept there, right? And *she* was under age too, when it happened. It would come out, you know, Dan, it would all have to come out."

"You could go to prison for this." The words came slowly out of Deacon's mouth, as though he were being half-throttled. "When I get hold of this man you've hired and prove his connection with you, you'll go to prison."

"If there were such a man, if I pretend for a minute that I know what you're talking about, then you can be sure that he'd be out of your reach. You'd never find him." Ocky took a cigar case, offered it to Deacon, selected a cigar himself, removed the band, lit up, puffed. "No, Dan, as I see it, you're the one who's likely to go to prison. In any case, think of the effect a case would have on Bella, and on your boys. Did you want to say something?"

In Deacon's mind there rose obscenities. He felt as though the blood in his veins were truly boiling with impotent anger. He shook his head.

"Now I've got to tell you that there's a further complication. These photographs were in Francie Lake's flat last night."

"Francie Lake? Oh, yes, Francie Lake."

"Whoever killed her took them. I've stalled the police by telling them that they were a different set of photographs. The point is this. These pictures in themselves don't mean much. They're only important to anyone who knows exactly where you were, and when. I believe they've been taken as a blind. But supposing the police knew about them, who had a motive for taking them? Why, you, Dan, nobody else."

Ocky was almost enveloped in blue smoke. Deacon was ordinarily a decisive man, but he felt physically numbed. "What do you want?"

"What I've always wanted. I want you to come in."

"If I come in," Deacon said, formulating the situation slowly, "What guarantee should I have of safety?"

"We might get a statement from Joe Mycock saying that you had paid him a visit after all. I'd turn over to you the names of the hotel people. But really, they're no threat to you."

"You mean you're the threat?"

"I wouldn't even say that." Ocky waved the end of his cigar thoughtfully. "The threat is in the whole thing, when you put it together. The Gwyneth business alone, well, you could say you were an innocent party, and supported her out of the goodness of your heart. The hotel business alone, well, you might be able to wriggle out of it if you could show you were somewhere else. The photographs alone don't mean much, as I've said. But put it all together, and it looks very nasty. And I'm the only person who can put it together. See what I mean?"

Before Deacon could answer a key turned in the lock, there was a voice in the hall, Bella entered the room. "Why, Dan, you're home early. And Ocky, what a nice surprise."

Ocky put down his cigar, rose, kissed her hand.

"Sometimes I think all these funds are really rackets just run by the organisers for the expenses. But I'd better not say that to you, Ocky, or you'll be asking me to find the evidence so that you can use it on TV or in your paper."

"He doesn't need any help in finding the evidence," Deacon said.

Bella looked from one to the other of them. "Anyway, I think I should have been better off at my reducing class. But I'm in the way."

"He was just going." Deacon's face might have been made out of wood.

Ocky beamed. "So I was. I've been trying to persuade Dan to come in with me on *The Plain Man*. Don't you think he should?"

"I never interfere. I've got no influence on him."

"Oh, I think you have. Hasn't she, Dan?"

"I'll let you know my decision."

"Don't leave it too long. Within the next forty-eight hours, shall we say?"

"Yes."

Ocky went. They saw him outside, bouncing jauntily into the Rolls. Levitt closed the door, got into the driver's seat, moved away. Bella was at the window.

"Such a sweet little man." She turned round. "Dan, what's the matter?"

"He's a crook." Her husband pounded with one fist on his open palm, and the effect was the more startling because he made very little sound, and the voice in which he spoke was as controlled as usual. The words he spoke were conventional, but they frightened her. "A dirty little low-down thieving crook. He's the lowest thing that crawls."

"But Dan, you've always known Ocky wasn't on the straight and narrow, as you might say."

"He is never to come into this house again."

"What does he want?"

"He wants to ruin us." He kissed her on the forehead, went out of the room and shut himself up in his study.

Chapter Sixteen

Francie Lake had a mother still living, and two brothers. They attended the official obsequies which were held later with benefit of clergy. But for years they had not been part of her life, and a truer obituary might have been obtained that Wednesday evening at the *British Volunteer*. There were a dozen people gathered around when Jimmy Crundle raised his pint of bitter and said solemnly, "To Francie."

They all drank. Lightfoot, the editor of *Whizz-O*, the children's paper, said, "She was close to the chief, wasn't she? He'll miss her."

"We shall all miss her."

"Just yesterday evening," Dex said, "she was sitting on her stool there, talking and drinking as she always did. You could trust Francie. She was a real trouper."

They missed her sadly, in great draughts of bitter. Boy Kirton was waiting for Jennifer Masterson. He felt a spasm of distaste rise in his mouth like bile. "It was only last night that she was calling us all zombies. The living dead. Remember?"

"Boy, Boy." Dex shook his head reprovingly.

Jimmy Crundle thrust forth his red face. "That's a bloody awful thing to say."

"It's the truth. That's what *The Plain Man* sets out to do, isn't it, tell the truth?"

"Right every time, Boy," Dex said. "Bang on the nose. Without fear or favour. Dedicated."

Boy Kirton felt like an actor who has played his part for a long time, and finds that the words he has been speaking automatically on the stage night by night are issuing from his mouth by day, so that life itself has taken on the artificiality of the stage. "Dedicated, shall I tell you one of the things we're dedicated to, the acutely intelligent criminologically highly trained staff of *Crime Today*?" Jack Smedley, on the outside of the group, bowed clumsily. "Finding Francie's killer, no less. Noses to the ground, bloodhounds, sniff me a strangler. Mary, more of this wallop all round please, and pour yourself a pint of these bitter tears as well."

"A drop of gin if you don't mind, Mr Kirton."

"Gin or beer, what does it matter how we mourn her? Her mourners will be outcast men, as Oscar says in what Dex might call the Rallad of Bedding Jail. Not that I mean *you're* an outcast, Mary, or that you've ever been rallad on the bedding."

Mary was plump and cheerful. "Half the time I don't understand what you mean, Mr Kirton, and perhaps it's as well. God bless Miss Lake, though."

"Circulationwise it's a good idea."

The bile was strong in his mouth. "As Mouseman says, golden lads and girls all must, like tarts and ponces, come to lust."

Pigeon-footed, shabby, silent, Ray Pillin was in their midst. "The first victim for interrogation," Boy Kirton said. "Developer of pictures, discoverer of corpus delinquent. What were you doing really in that flat this morning, what are those stains I see on your clothes? Don't make an obscene answer, I want the truth, Pillin. Where Scotland Yard grilled you I shall fry, where they gave you three degrees I shall give five."

"A bitter, miss."

"That's a bloody awful thing to say."

"Jack Smedley was tugging at Kirton's elbow. "Not here, Boy. There's a time and place."

"Bloody awful," Jimmy Crundle repeated. "To say a thing like that."

"We all had our spats with Francie, but she was a fine woman." That was Lightfoot.

"I remember once when she was looking through a feature I'd done – "

"What about those photographs?" Kirton shook off Jack Smedley's hand, looked at his watch, put his own hand on Pillin's jacket. The jacket felt greasy, fingers slipped over it. "What were they?" Pillin gulped desperately at his beer. "None of that can't stay for an answer caper, what?"

Pillin put down his glass. "Hasn't the chief told you?"

"I want to hear it from you."

"Army pictures, running at the double with full pack, all that sort of stuff." The little face looked up, frightened, into his.

"Bloody awful." Now Pillin's body was shoved roughly aside, replaced by Jimmy Crundle's. "No decency, no reverence. Just don't know what it means. Little Francie only a few hours in her grave, and you – "

"She's not in her grave."

Crundle aimed a wild roundhouse swing which Kirton could easily have evaded. In that instant, however, he saw, on the fringe of their group Jennifer Masterson, her blue eyes wide and puzzled. The blow caught him on the side of the head. Flushed with success Jimmy struck again, a great looped uppercut that caught Kirton on the chin.

He felt his body jarred, as though he had been walking along in darkness and had come into contact with some obstacle, an iron stanchion, say. Then he was lifted off the ground, a sensation that was in itself not unpleasant. After that he was aware of noise, an intolerable noise going on in his head. At the same time the ground seemed to give way, and he thought that he must be involved in an earthquake.

The earthquake ended when he opened his eyes and found himself looking up at Jennifer Masterson. His face was wet.

Blood, he thought, and put a hand to it, but it proved to be water.

"Are you all right?"

He felt his jaw experimentally, looked round. The bar seemed to be empty. "Yes. Where is everybody?"

"I've turned them all out." Mary's face, displeased, hove into his field of vision. "Mr Crundle was struggling and swearing, it took three of them to hold him. Those that don't know how to behave after a drink or two should stay on the wagon."

"Give me a hand, will you." They gave him a hand each, and he got up. "Ouch."

"Now that you're up you can get out too. The landlord wanted to call the police, be thankful I talked him out of it. Miss Lake would have been ashamed."

"You're wrong there, Mary. She would have been amused." Outside, he sniffed up the damp October air. "That's better. I'm not in the least drunk. I thought you weren't going to turn up."

"I'm sorry. I was going to send a message. Then I thought you'd be having a drink and it didn't matter."

"It didn't. I hope they get Jimmy home all right, he can be very wild. Shall we have dinner?"

"I'm not hungry."

They walked up Fleet Street, through the Temple, sat down. The evening was misty, damp and warm. "You were arguing about Francie Lake. She was the general manager, wasn't she?"

"If you call it arguing."

"I saw her in the pub last night. She didn't look very nice."

"Nice?" He rolled the word around in his mind. "Perhaps not. But there was something about her, I don't know what you'd call it. Honesty, perhaps."

She smiled at him, and the ghost of Elaine flickered between them. "It's a word that seems to worry you. Isn't it just a matter of toughness, really?"

"No, it's what it does to you over the years, and not so many years at that. Francie was Ocky's girlfriend at one time. I don't

101

think she ever got over it. You might say none of us has ever got over Ocky."

The lights shone above them, turning her fair hair mauve. On the Embankment traffic rattled past. He had a quite illusionary vision of himself in a state of innocence walking here years ago with Elaine, illusory because he had never walked here with Elaine, their life together had been lived for the most part in crowded rooms, among friends and casual acquaintances, the clatter of conversation surrounding them always. "You remind me of my wife."

"I didn't know you had one."

"I haven't. She was killed four years ago. In a car accident. I was driving." She said nothing. "I'm not asking for sympathy."

"You mean you are. But you won't get it. That's not a good reason for taking girls out to dinner, because they remind you of your dead wife. Why do they call you Boy?"

"It started years ago."

"I don't like it," she said vehemently. "You've got a name, people ought to use it. What is it?"

"Charles."

"Not much of a name, but I shall use it. She came to our house a couple of days ago."

He was startled. "Who did?"

"Francie Lake. I recognised her in the pub last night. She came to see my father."

"What for?"

"I don't know. She was only at the house a few minutes."

He thought about it. Perhaps Francie had gone to see Masterson on some business of Ocky's, but it was unlike Ocky to trust anything serious to anybody else, even to Francie. "She wasn't carrying papers, a brief-case, anything like that?"

"I didn't notice. Do you think it's important? It seems queer, that's all."

"Shall I ask father?"

So simple a solution had not occurred to him. "Would he tell you?"

"I'm his favourite daughter. And he can only say no."

"Ask him, then." He stood up. "Come back to my flat. I'll scramble some eggs and make some coffee."

She shook her head. "That's not why you want me to go back."

He considered. "I suppose not. You won't?"

"If you hadn't told me about your wife, I might. But I don't want to have a ghost between us when we're making love. You're sorry enough for yourself already, that would make it worse."

"Will you come out with me tomorrow evening?"

"Won't you be engaged in criminal investigation?"

"Oh, that." He was dismissive. "It's an idea of Ocky's, that's all."

"I'll ask daddy what Miss Lake wanted. After all, if it's anything important I suppose he'll tell the police, so why shouldn't he tell me? Good night."

She waved her hand and walked away, tall and loosely elegant. He watched until she turned the corner, and was conscious that after all he felt extremely hungry. He went to Lyons and ate a steak and salad. His jaw was tender when he ate. Otherwise he felt extremely well.

Chapter Seventeen

On the following morning Sergeant Quick reported the results of his preliminary investigations to Superintendent Nevers.

"We've done a good deal of talking to the neighbours, the boys and I, but without much luck. There are two flats above hers. The couple on the first floor are away he's some sort of engineer, gone off for a couple of days, his wife's staying with friends. The couple on the top floor, artist and his wife, didn't hear anything out of the way. Ditto the neighbours next door and opposite. One of the neighbours saw her come home in a taxi just before eight o'clock. A man got out of it, saw her in and drove off."

"That was Stead, works at the firm."

"Is that so, sir."

"I talked to Stead this afternoon. He seemed nervous. Told me he'd taken her home, dropped her off, then gone to the cinema. I wondered why he was nervous."

"Talking to a superintendent?"

Nevers smiled, but wrote the name "Stead" on a pad. "Go on, Quick."

"Somebody else saw Pillin arrive and leave just about the time he said, ten-thirty. This was a woman standing in the street saying goodbye to a friend. After that, nothing. There's a back entrance to the house through an alley, same key as the one at the front. May have come in that way, nobody would be likely to notice."

"Pity. What else?"

"General impressions. People in central London aren't neighbourly, not what I call neighbourly. Everybody knew her by sight, not many to talk to. She seems to have had several men friends, and there's a suggestion from some old cow across the road that they sometimes stayed the night. Oh, and while we're on the subject of men, we've had a chance to go through those letters. A lot of them are from Gaye himself, and it's obvious the two of them were very close way back in the past. I don't mean just that she was his mistress, but – well, you know, they were interested in the same things, wanted the same things, you can see that." Quick, who had in a mild way a literary turn of mind, said, "Very interesting letters they are."

"But not recent."

"Lord, no, five years old or more. There's a bunch of photographs of them together, but they're all old stuff as well, mementoes. Quite a lot of other letters from men, but again nothing very recent. Desk – nothing of interest there, mostly bills, a bit of office stuff, nothing personal. I should think you'd find out more about her by talking to people at the office."

"Yes, and no. I talked yesterday to all the heads of departments and the people most closely associated with her. They all said she was tough, efficient, hard to get along with at times, but no more so than you'd expect. Never put on airs, always one of the boys, went across the road and had a drink with them when the day's work was done. One or two of them were a bit afraid of her, regarded her as Gaye's voice, but I shouldn't say they were covering up anything. I get the impression that she played the cards pretty close to her chest always. Gaye himself – " He hesitated.

"Yes?"

"Didn't really add much to the picture. Said she was his right-hand woman and all that, told me about their affair, said it was all over long ago." Nevers still felt that in some way he had been bamboozled by Ocky. Vengefully he said, "He's a slippery customer."

Quick did not comment. He felt that he would have handled Ocky Gaye better than the super.

"He confirmed what Pillin told us about those photos, said they came from a soldier named Patterson, who'd got a photographer chum to take them. Strickland's been down to Patterson's unit, seen him, and got out of him that they did take some pictures and smuggled them out to Gaye. Only thing is, he says they gave Gaye the negatives a week ago, and I got the impression he'd only just received them. You might have another little chat with Master Pillin."

"Yes, sir. We found Pillin's prints on the photographs that were lying around, but then he admitted he handled them. A good many other prints, too, but we can't tell if they're significant."

"Anything more on that letter?"

"Nothing. I've got the feeling it's a fake, though why the chap who killed her should have written at such length I don't know. He could have established his point about the time and then written three or four lines, no need to go into all that rigmarole about the colour of the sky." He paused. "There are no leads from the office, except Stead. Go and see him, will you, see what you make of him."

"At the office?" Quick said eagerly and Nevers laughed.

"If you like. Probe around a bit, find out if he was antagonistic to her, whether she'd threatened to get him the sack. Then I want to know more about her personal life. Gaye says it was a bit rackety, picking up men in night clubs and taking them home. Nobody else seems to know much of what she did outside the office. Put a couple of men on to night clubs. What's the matter?"

"There was a box of matches in her bag. It came from a club called the Double Trouble. Mayfair."

"Respectable?"

"Don't know anything against it."

"Right then, take a picture of her with you, start with the Double Trouble, then nose round the office."

"Would you like me to see Gaye?"

"No, thank you. I know you'd like to pay your respects, Quick, but Gaye's a busy man. He's got a crusade for the underdog to carry on. We don't want to worry him unnecessarily now, do we? But look after the clubs. This is a feast for the nationals. We don't want some crime reporter coming up with a scoop."

Chapter Eighteen

The Double Trouble was near Marble Arch, just off Bryanston Street. A notice outside said Double Trouble Club. Strictly private. Members Only. Quick went down a passage and found a smooth-haired young man at the end of it.

"You a member?"

Quick showed his card and asked for Mr Rockingham.

"I'll see if he's in."

"I'll see too." The young man shrugged his shoulders and led him through a bar where two men were drinking, into a large dining-room. At most of the tables groups of business men sat eating lunch, but some of the other tables were occupied by single men and women. They were served by waitresses wearing what seemed to be the top half of a nurse's uniform. The lower half had been replaced by a skirt that ended at the top of the thighs. In the middle of the room there was a small dais, and as Quick and the young man walked across the room a girl moved past them and on to this dais. She was naked except for a cache-sexe, and as she stood on the dais it began slowly to revolve. The business men stopped eating, looked at her consideringly, then went back to their steaks. Quick stood and stared. After perhaps a minute the dais stopped revolving, and the girl walked off.

At the end of the restaurant the young man pulled aside a curtain, tapped on a door, and closed it before Quick could stop him. Then he opened it again and jerked a thumb. Quick went in.

The room was comfortable, but not luxurious. The man who rose to greet him was fair-haired, and pretty as a doll. He was about Quick's own age. He wore a Guards' tie, and had a ready smile.

"Don't think we know each other, old man, do we? My name's Rockingham. What have we been doing wrong?"

"I don't know that you've done anything. That's a very unusual floor show you have out there."

"Aid to the digestion. Nothing more, old man, I can assure you of that. We're very respectable here."

"I wanted a little information." Rockingham, nodded. Quick produced Francie's photograph. "Do you know who this is?"

"Yes. Francie Lake. You want to know about her?"

"Everything, yes, please."

"Have a cigarette, old man? No? Well, I will." Now perfectly at ease, Rockingham crossed one elegant leg over another. "She came here quite a lot, Francie, and I often used to talk to her. I felt sorry for her, underneath that hard crust she was just a little girl lost, if you know what I mean. Or perhaps she wasn't lost, but she was looking for something. She'll never find it now."

"How often did she come in?"

"Sometimes twice a week, even more perhaps, sometimes not for three or four weeks. Mostly alone. We've got a telephone system, sort of thing they used in the good old days in Berlin, you see someone you like the look of, you ask a waitress for her number, ring her and ask if she'd like to join you. Nothing wrong about it, the girl can always say no, but of course most of the girls who come in here alone are – well, you know. Now, Francie came here alone, as I say, but she wasn't really – "

"She wasn't a tart, you mean."

"You're being crude, old man, and you're not even right." Rockingham, looked positively disapproving. "I wouldn't allow that sort of thing. No, what I meant is that most of the girls who come in alone do it for the thrill. They want to go with a strange man, someone they don't know at all. You know."

"No, I don't think I do."

"It's not important, anyway, except that Francie wasn't like that."

"You mean she never picked up a man in here?"

"I wish you wouldn't talk like that," Rockingham said pettishly. "But never mind. For one thing, not many men telephoned Francie – she was no chicken, you know – and for another, as like as not she wouldn't join them when they did. And then occasionally she'd telephone a man herself, ask him to have a drink. That's very unusual, you know. She was unusual, Francie. Only a few nights ago we were having a drink and I said to her, 'Francie, dear, what are you looking for, what are you trying to prove?' But she wouldn't tell me, I don't think she really knew."

"Were there any particular men she came here with?"

"One or two, but I couldn't tell you their names. I mean, I don't know them." Rockingham smiled sweetly. "And there were quite a few she met and talked to here, but it didn't mean anything."

"She didn't go off with them?"

"She may have done, I don't know. The sort of people who come in here expect discretion and they get it. But the point is, they didn't matter to Francie. She was a lonely person. There was somebody she came in with quite often, though, recently. Younger than she was, dark, wore fancy waistcoats. Good looking."

"When did she last come in here?"

"Today's Thursday, it would have been Monday. She came in alone and I bought her a drink. She seemed gayer than usual, more relaxed. I like to see people relaxed." He smiled slightly. "She said something to me about it never being too late to start again."

"Can you remember the exact words?"

"It went something like this, old man. 'It's a mistake ever to think you're finished, Rocky, you can always shape life the way you want it if you're strong enough. It's a matter of the will.' I don't know if that makes any sense to you old man, I can't say it did to me, but I said I was pleased she was happy. She stayed an hour or so, then her young man picked her up and they left together."

Quick tried to get a more exact description of Francie's companion, but had no luck. When he left, Rockingham came out into the restaurant with him. He walked with easy grace. Another girl moved past them on her way to the dais. Quick's head moved round to follow her.

"You wouldn't care to be my guest for lunch?"

"No, thank you."

"It *is* rather boring at this time of day." Quick noticed a man pick up one of the tiny telephones hooked on to the tables, and speak into it. "Look in one evening, old man. Ask for me. I'd love to see you."

Eating his lunch of sandwiches in a snack bar, Quick thought ruefully of the old adage: virtue is its own reward, it has no others.

Chapter Nineteen

Jimmy Crundle came into Boy Kirton's office looking cheerful. He wore a dashing suit in small red and black checks, his red face was beautifully shaved. His teeth, as he opened his mouth in a broad smile, were perfectly white. Below, beneath, behind the smell of after-shave lotion was an odour of food and tobacco, an overpowering male scent.

"I hear you're having a new name on the door, Sleuths Incorporated or the New Sherlock." Kirton smiled unenthusiastically. Jimmy thrust out a hand. "Boy, I've come in to say I'm sorry. They tell me I took a poke at you last night, I don't remember it, I just didn't know what I was doing. You can tell that. Boy, hell, if I ever took a poke at anybody it wouldn't be you. Why is it that when I fly off the handle it has to be with my best friends?"

There seemed to be no answer. He accepted the outstretched hand. "No damage done."

"I'm glad to hear it." Jimmy spoke as seriously as if Kirton had been the victim of a street accident. "I tell you, Anna really tore off a strip when I got home last night. She says I must go on the water wagon. And she's right, Boy, she's right."

Kirton had heard this before. He played with a paper knife and said nothing. Jimmy's euphoria flowed unchecked.

"This is a terrific idea of Ocky's, tracking down poor Francie's killer through the organisation. I reckon we can really make something of it tomorrow night on the programme. We're

112

holding over the piece we'd done, filmed stuff about old age pensioners, we'll do your team live instead, making an investigation. On the spot stuff. I've got to talk it over with the producer, but this is the way I see it. We introduce Ocky as usual, and he says a bit about Francie, then announces he's devoting the whole programme to the investigation. Cut to you in Francie's office holding up a picture of her, saying something like this: 'This was Francie Lake, who was found stabbed to death in her own flat early on Wednesday morning. My name is Charles Kirton, and I'm editor of *Crime Today*, one of the magazines in the Plain Man group. Under Mr Gaye's direction we're making an inquiry into all the circumstances.' Are you with me?" Kirton nodded. Jimmy rubbed his chin. "After that it's difficult. You'll have to say something about our investigation not conflicting with police inquiries, that's important. I think the best way of handling the thing would be to follow Francie's activities on that Tuesday night. Such and such a time she left the office and went into the *British Volunteer*, seemed much as usual."

"She wasn't quite as usual, she was talking about zombies and so on."

"I wasn't there, Boy, took Anna to a theatre. All right, we say she seemed a bit nervous. Bring on Bill Stead to say he took her home in a taxi, everything okay. Then there's Pillin, he was the last person to see her alive, but I don't think he'd make the right impression, better to have you telling 'em about it. *Then* we go inside her flat."

"Shall we be allowed to do that?"

"Ocky will fix it. Besides, what are we doing but helping the police? All right with you?"

"I suppose so."

"That's just a rough outline, of course. Later today I shall want some filmed stuff of investigators investigating, talking to Francie's neighbours, that sort of thing. We'll cut them in and have Ocky do a commentary on them, what do you say?"

"Yes. Talk to Jack Smedley about it, will you."

When Jimmy had gone, Kirton left his room and walked along the corridor to the door that said *Miss F. Lake, General Manager.* The room was almost a duplicate of his own, the same big window, the same sort of desk with the same telephones on it, the same small cupboard. He went to the cupboard, opened it, saw the swagger coat hanging there, and felt pity for the dead. He sat down at the desk, opened the drawers, began to look through the papers, idly and without expectation of finding anything. He turned over copies of memos, neatly and tightly written, to Dex, to Jimmy, Lightfoot, himself, each one a model of concision. Then there was another file of memos to Ocky. Looking through these, memos summarising and advising on projects, warning of dangers, clarifying ideas that had been clumsily put, he realised how she had tied together all the strings of the organisation, how clearly and surely she had grasped what was going on. In the desk drawers, though, there was nothing more personal than an old lipstick and a packet of Kleenex. He turned unexpectantly to the trays of correspondence on the desk. Here again there was nothing but the impersonal face that Francie Lake had presented to the world. He was putting back these papers when one that had become attached by a paper clip to a memorandum fluttered out and down to the carpet.

He picked up the piece of paper. It was a fragment torn off a larger sheet, and contained nothing but the name Daniel Deacon. A letter Deacon had signed, perhaps – but why tear off his signature? He took the paper over to the window and held it against the light. Behind the firm signature, written in blue ink, another colour – violet, perhaps – was faintly discernible.

He was still at the window when the desk buzzer sounded. He shivered, walked across and picked up the instrument.

"There you are," Ocky said. "Mercury's been looking for you all over, said you must be out of the office. Just one of my touches of inspiration to realise you might be investigating. Come in."

When he entered Ocky's office the little man was jubilant. "You can go and have a look at Francie's flat. Nevers has agreed to it. Under a little pressure I may say. I had to go higher up." He winked. "It would be a scandal if *The Plain Man* were prevented from assisting the cause of justice, don't you agree? And we can film in the flat tomorrow night."

"Good."

"Have a look round this afternoon, see what's doing. Take Jimmy with you. And keep yourself free for lunch, Boy, we'll have a bite in Boulestin's and talk about the way it should be done. We can make this something really good."

Chapter Twenty

"I understand." Deverston was a little lean man with a long sharp nose.

"I'm not sure you do, but it doesn't matter," Deacon said. "just go over it again."

"A hotel somewhere near Paddington."

"Try within a half-mile radius. And remember, it can't be very reputable."

"Between seven and eight o'clock Tuesday night. A man who looked like you, and a girl. Registered as Mr and Mrs Dai Davies. A row in the hotel. The manager and desk clerk are the two people involved."

"Right."

"Once I've found what hotel it is, you just want me to report back to you."

"Right."

Deverston said hesitantly, "It's not my business. But if I don't find the hotel and there's a lot of shady hotels round there, this sounds like a blackmail job. If you take my advice, tell them to go to hell."

"I don't need advice."

The expression on Deacon's face was such that Deverston thought: I shouldn't like to be the one trying to put the black on him. Aloud he said, "I'll use three men on it, Sir Daniel. And report twice a day."

Left alone, Deacon wondered if Gaye had really slipped up and told the truth when he said that the hotel was near Paddington. If he had there was a good chance of finding it. Anyway, it was worth trying.

Chapter Twenty-One

Quick enjoyed going to Fleet Street, was prepared to gawk like any country boy at the vision of grandeur presented by the marble entrance hall of Plain Man Enterprises, with its grave commissionaires, its boys rushing urgently about, its mural showing a St. George of the Press grappling with a creature whose various heads bore such names as *Bureaucratic Spender*, *Uncivil Servant, Trade Union Tyrant*. He learned that Mr Stead was to be found in Room 110. He was walking across to the lift when he sensed a change in the attitudes of the people in the hall, rather as though they had been given a brief galvanising shock. He turned. Ocky Gaye had just come in from the street.

It was rarely that Ocky walked through the entrance hall without a word of greeting to some of the people there. Perhaps it was some special sense that made him say to Quick, "I'm Ocky Gaye. Can I help you?"

Quick swallowed hard. Seen at close quarters Ocky was, he thought, even more impressive than on the magic screen. The large blue-grey eyes looked at him encouragingly, the whole easy manner suggested that he had all the time in the world to spare for your problem, and that this problem would be made his exclusive interest. Quick showed Ocky his card.

"Oh, yes. It's about poor Francie, then. Do you want to see me? By the way, this is Mr Kirton, one of my chief executives."

The man standing behind Ocky, who was good looking and youthful, but slightly haggard, nodded.

"I've come to see Mr Stead, as a matter of fact. But if you could spare me five minutes – "

"Of course. Come this way." They went up, the three of them, in his private lift, and walked along a corridor. Behind its glass partitions Quick felt, or imagined, the pulsation of the great Fleet Street heart. At one of the doors Kirton stopped. Ocky said, "Keep in touch, Boy, I'm always available." As they walked on and turned a corner. Ocky talked.

"A wonderful lad, Boy Kirton, came to me straight from university, trust him like nobody else now that Francie's gone."

Now they were in the office and Quick was overwhelmed by the size of it, by the bust and the dashing John portrait. He accepted a cigar, he had a drink, he listened while Ocky told him about the investigation. "No reflection on the police, you understand that, this is just an attempt to help in our own small way. Francie had been with me since the very first issue of the paper – I don't know if you ever see it – "

Quick bought it every week. Ocky expressed himself immensely gratified.

"Then you know what it means to me, and what it meant to Francie. I should think I was failing in my duty if I didn't try to find out who killed her." Admonitory finger raised. "We shall turn over anything we find out to Superintendent Nevers, naturally."

"I'm glad to hear you say that." Quick heard the fervent note in his own voice, and gathered wits dazed by cigar and drink. "Tell me, Mr Gaye, did Miss Lake ever say anything about leaving you?"

The blue-grey eyes stared at him astonished. "She certainly didn't."

"Because she was talking vaguely about starting a new life, saying it was never too late and so on."

Ocky shook his head. "I can't believe she'd ever have left. She helped to build this place, she was part of its blood and bones if you'll forgive the mixed metaphor. In a business way we were

119

still very close, though we'd drifted apart personally. I don't know much about her personal life in the last year or two. I should say she was a lonely woman."

It was what Rockingham had said, but it did not seem to be of much help. Unwillingly Quick rose from his chair. Ocky accompanied him to the door. Quick found a washroom, and saw that he was still smoking the cigar. The effect was slightly ludicrous. He stubbed it out and then went along to Room 110, which said *William Stead. Complaints.*

The room was small. A man sat in it at a desk piled high with papers. As he rose to greet Quick, the sergeant saw that he was dark, and that beneath his dark blue jacket he wore a lighter blue flowered waistcoat.

It was a good thing in general not to theorise in advance of your facts, but Quick felt instinctively that this was an occasion when a leap in the dark might be justified. He said abruptly, "Sergeant Quick, CID."

"Yes?" Stead was very pale.

"I wanted to ask some further questions about your relationship with Miss Lake. I believe you were friendly."

"Who told you? Never mind, I suppose you've got to know. Yes, we were friendly, if that's what you want to call it. She'd been my mistress."

"You're married, Mr Stead? I thought so. You say she had been your mistress. You mean it was all over?"

"I'd told her it must end. I love my wife."

"And had Miss Lake accepted this idea?"

"She would have had to accept it. That was the way it had to be."

"What was her attitude?"

In a voice hardly above a whisper, Stead said, "She wanted me to divorce my wife, and marry her."

"Did your wife know about this relationship?"

"No. She may have suspected, but she didn't know."

"Although you say you were breaking with Miss Lake, you met her at the Double Trouble club on Monday night."

"We had a lot to talk over."

"And then on Tuesday night you took her home to her flat."

"Yes. She was feeling pretty low. I didn't go in."

"Did you go back there later?"

"No, I didn't. Look, will my wife, have to know about this?"

"I couldn't say. I suggest you come down now to headquarters and make a complete statement about your association with Miss Lake. Get it down officially. If you tell me the details here, you'll only have to make a statement later. What about it?"

"All right. I'll just tell my secretary I have to be out for an hour. Will that be long enough?"

"Better make it a couple of hours."

Chapter Twenty-Two

I have known Francie Lake for eighteen months, ever since I came to work on *The Plain Man.* I saw quite a lot of her at first, because I worked on the editorial side, in which she took a great interest. I didn't altogether like some of the work I was doing, and she arranged that I should be transferred to the Complaints Department. The Department doesn't deal only with complaints about the paper, but with abuses brought to us by readers who are asking for help. When Gerrish, the head of the department, had a stroke and retired, I was promoted, and I felt that I owed this to her. She had a great deal of authority.

She often talked about my work when we were having a drink together in the *British Volunteer,* and told me not to make any mistake, we were doing important and useful work, although I gathered she thought we were off our proper course as a reforming paper at some times, and that this was largely due to Mr Gaye. About nine months ago she asked me to go out to dinner with her, and I agreed. It was shortly afterwards that she became my mistress, and the relationship has lasted until the present time, more or less. I say "more or less" because I have several times told her that I wanted to break it off, but in fact we never did so. About three months ago she suggested that I should divorce my wife, Mary, and that we should get married.

I refused, but she did not really accept the refusal. She said I would change my mind.

She was a very secretive woman. She insisted that nobody in the office should know about our relationship. She said that it would be bad for office morale, but I don't think this was her only reason. As far as I know, nobody did know about it. She also seemed to be a very lonely person. She told me that she used to go to a restaurant club called the Double Trouble and try to pick up a man there so that she could take him home with her. She said it was companionship she wanted as much as anything else, and really that was what she wanted from me too. I felt sorry for her, but she was much older than me, and after a time I felt I didn't want to be entangled.

As far as I know, my wife knew nothing about my relationship with Francie, but she did know that something was wrong. We were getting on badly, and she spoke of leaving me.

Last Monday I met Francie by arrangement, in the Double Trouble. I didn't like her to go there, but she seemed to be fascinated by the place. She was in high spirits, and seemed to think that I had not been serious about breaking off our relationship. We went out to dinner, and she talked about leaving the organisation and setting up some sort of publicity business together. Later on, she said, we could get married. I told her hat I had no intention of marrying her, and that I thought we should make a clean break. She was very much upset. We parted at about eleven o'clock. When I got home my wife said that she felt sure I had been with another woman and that she was leaving me.

On Tuesday my wife came round to the *British Volunteer,* and there was a slight scene in the bar when I refused to leave the bar with her. She left, and has not returned home. I believe she is staying with her sister. I left the *British Volunteer* with Francie, and took her home. It was about eight o'clock when we got to her flat. I did not go in. I did not see her again or return to the flat. I went home, found that my wife was not there and went out drinking. I returned to my own home at about eleven-thirty that night, and did not go out again.

"What do you think?" Quick asked Nevers, when Stead had gone. "Is he telling the truth?"

"Part of it, perhaps. At least he's given us a motive of sorts. Francie is going to break up happy home, so he kills her. But I feel there's more to come. We'll go on digging."

Chapter Twenty-Three

Kirton shivered as he entered the flat, not with cold. Jimmy Crundle pushed ahead of him, entered the sitting-room.

"They've left the set-up just as it was, even the old chalk marks on the floor. What have we got? Lounge, yes, and here's the old bath and lav and behind this door the abode of Morpheus."

"How do you know?"

Jimmy stared. "I've been in for the odd drink once or twice. Haven't you?"

"No."

"It could be Francie was a wee bit jealous of your influence with our lord and master, I'm not sure you were her favourite person."

"She had relatives, hadn't she? Francie, I mean. What are they going to think?"

"Ocky's done it all, Boy, spoken to her mother and one of her brothers, and they are perfectly and absolutely happy about the whole affair, a great tribute to Francie, etcetera. It's all tied up."

With a spasm of irritation he said, "I thought you were talking last night about decency and reverence."

Jimmy looked injured. He was sweating. "You've certainly got the needle today, Boy."

"Don't call me Boy. I've got a name." He turned on his heel before Jimmy could reply, and went into the bedroom. There was something immeasurably sad about the apparatus of a life laid out here, the bed that still bore a body's print, the powder and lipstick on the dressing-table.

"Just as it was." Jimmy stood in the doorway. "That's perfect. Don't see any real problems. You talk first in the lounge, then you come in here."

Kirton was not listening. He was looking at a little pamphlet that lay face down beside the bed. It was called the *Criminal Guide* and it was a kind of catalogue issued monthly by a London bookseller, giving details of out-of-date books on criminology. Kirton subscribed to it, because the books were frequently useful for confecting *Crime Today* articles. He had received his copy of the latest issue, by post, on Tuesday morning.

"What are you looking at?"

Kirton showed him. "I didn't know Francie subscribed to this thing."

"Perhaps she didn't. Bought it at a bookstall, perhaps."

"It's for subscribers only. I got my copy on Tuesday morning."

"All right, then, Francie was a subscriber after all."

"I'm sure she wasn't. What interest would it have for her?"

"Search me. If you ask me it means strictly nothing."

"I only know one other subscriber in the office. That's Bill Stead. He worked on *Crime Today* when he first came to us, I remember he was collecting Victorian detective stories and he took the *Criminal Guide* for that."

"Is that so?" Jimmy was not interested. "Let's get down to cases. You begin in here…"

When they left the flat Jimmy went off to talk to the television producer, McClintock, and Kirton returned to the office. Dex and Jack Smedley were talking in the room that housed *Crime Today*. Dex greeted him warmly.

"Just the chap. We're going to run a *Plain Man* feature on your search for the murderer. Jack here's been telling me about the set-up, retracing Francie's steps, investigations in the office, all that caper. But we shall want a piece from you, not long, three or four hundred words, saying how you're deploying your forces and all that. Publicitywise it should be useful."

He looked at their two smiling faces. "Factwise, it's a phoney."

"Oh, come on now, Boy. I'm just doing my job."

"Jobwise I can see it's necessary. But you know it's a phoney, why not say so out loud to me. Go on, say it. You can whisper if you like." He offered an ear.

Dex looked offended. "A joke's a joke, but there is such a thing as going too far."

"All right. I suppose you'll want some pictures. Is Ray Pillin around? I want to talk to him."

"The chief's sent him on leave for a few days. He was upset, Pillin, I mean. Must have been a shock to him."

Kirton grunted. The irritation he felt was almost more than he could bear. The door opened. Jennifer Masterson stood in the doorway. He waved her in.

"All right, Dex, I'll do those three hundred words and you can send the photographers round, we'll put on a show. Now, I'm busy." He walked into his own small office and Jennifer followed him. Dex and Jack Smedley stared after them.

"I shouldn't have interrupted. I just wanted you to know that I spoke to daddy early this morning. He wouldn't say anything at first, except that it was confidential. But in the end he told me it was all about some forms of guarantee."

"A guarantee for Plain Man Enterprises?"

"Not exactly. It was for what daddy called a holding company named Gaye Developments."

"Francie wanted to see these forms?"

"Yes, and she had a letter from Mr Gaye saying it was all right. So daddy showed them to her. The funny thing is – "

"Yes?"

"Daddy said it wasn't important, the guarantee form I mean. It was simply a renewal of a guarantee that had been issued each year."

"Was Sir Daniel Deacon one of the people who had signed it?"

"I don't know. Daddy didn't say. Oh, yes, he laughed and said he had signed the guarantee himself, and all the other people who signed were equally respectable. After Miss Lake was killed he told the police about it, but they didn't seem to attach much importance to it. What do you think?"

"I don't know. Now I'll tell you something." He told her about the copy of the *Criminal Guide.*

She listened, frowning, then asked why he thought it was important. Francie would never have subscribed to a thing like that, she had no interest in it."

"Somebody lent it to her, or left it there."

"I got my copy on Tuesday morning. It's still in my desk. If all the copies were sent out at the same time – do you see what I mean?"

"It may have been left by her murderer."

"There's only one other person in the office who took the *Guide* so far as I know, and that's Bill Stead." He paused. "I'm going to see the man who runs the *Guide* this evening. Will you come with me?"

Chapter Twenty-Four

"The Camerons. Where are the Camerons?"

"What Camerons?" Mercury Ellis asked.

"Wake up, there. Jeannie Cameron, last week's programme, the family we rehoused, remember? I've rung Bill Stead and I get no answer. I want to know where he is. Find Dex and Jimmy Crundle and tell them to come in. Trouble is, all my assistants are living the good life. Have you bought that new frock?"

Mercury smiled. "I'm waiting until I get the next instalments of my rise."

Ocky growled at her with pretended ferocity. Three minutes later she told him: "Mr Stead went off with a sergeant from Scotland Yard. Mr Crundle is out with Mr Kirton. Mr Welcome was in production, and is just coming down. And here's the Cameron's address. It's a new estate, and they don't like it much."

"Good girl. I want to know how many letters we had about the Camerons after last week's programme. And tell Levitt I shall want the car. In ten minutes."

When Dex came in he found Ocky pacing up and down like a little bear. "Do you know how many letters we had from last week's programme, Dex? More than eight hundred, all complaining about housing conditions, asking us to set things right. And they're still coming in. What are we doing about it?"

"It's a bit difficult. Housing isn't a fresh issue, and with all the private building that's been going on these last few years I don't see that – "

"Not a fresh issue." Ocky's eyes were wide with horrified surprise. "Eight hundred letters come in and you say it's not a fresh issue. Don't you see that's only the fringe, there are tens of thousands, hundreds of thousands of people all living in misery in our so called Welfare State? And you say we should do nothing about it."

"We can't rehouse them all."

"Can't we, though? What's wrong with building houses ourselves and rehousing a thousand people on The Plain Man Housing Estate?"

Dex goggled, then said feebly, "Moneywise, Chief, would it be practical?"

Ocky thumped the desk with his plump fist. "Vision, Dex, vision. Where there is no vision the people perish. I want these letters and all the others that are coming in read, analysed by area, type of complaint, income level, size of family and so on. Then I want a campaign in the paper featuring some of the worst cases. If it's not a fresh issue we'll make it one, we'll make all those petty bureaucrats in Whitehall shift their fat bottoms out of their chairs, we'll make the people of England understand who's on their side. And don't stand there casting your eyes up above like a parson in the pulpit, man, I mean what I'm saying."

There was no arguing with Ocky in this mood. "It'll take a few days to make the analysis."

Ocky brushed aside such petty details. "I'm going down now to see the Camerons. I want a photographer with me. If Consett is free I'll take him." He suddenly patted Dex on the shoulder. "You'll see, we shall make a real crusade out of this. The Housing Crusade."

The Camerons had been rehoused in one of the south-western suburbs. They had some difficulty in finding this particular new red brick house among what proved to be road after road of identical houses, all set well back from the wide road. At every turn there were notices which said "Children Playing – Careful" and "Admittance Only To Residents Of Estate" and "No Parking Here – Except For Residents." The Rolls created a gratifying amount of attention among the children playing in the patches of front garden. At last they found the house, and Ocky rang the bell. The door was opened by a militant looking woman wearing an apron. She glared at him, then the glare changed to a smile.

"It's Mr Gaye." She looked past him. "Have you brought the TV people? Oh, I see, just a photographer. Come in. I was making a cupper." She suddenly shrieked, "Jeannie."

Ocky followed her into a small sitting-room. Jeannie came in, followed by the children he remembered on the programme as looking unnaturally clean. They had subsided now into a more congenial grubbiness. He sat down and drank tea from a cup marked by other lips. "I just dropped in to see how you like it here."

Jeannie said quickly, "You've been wonderful to us, Mr Gaye, we shall never forget your kindness."

"Oh, Mr Gaye's been very *kind,*" her mother agreed. "He's been *kind,* no doubt about that."

"Is there something you don't like about the house?"

"Oh, the *house* is all right, very nice."

"Ask me, it's bloody awful here, and that's what Dad would say if he was home." This was Rickie, a menacing-looking youth who wore a bright shirt, a zip-fronted jacket with "Arabs" on front and back, and very tight jeans. He expanded. "They're all cissies here. Back home we used to have our gang, like I was in the Arabs and the Jew boys had their gang, and we'd fight them, see? Here it's – you just don't get any fun."

"They're so stuck up, our neighbours. They say we ought to go back where we came from," said Mrs Cameron. "Especially after they saw us on the TV. They said you had no right, putting us in here."

"But of course it's ever so nice, the house I mean. And there are no black people." That was Jeannie.

"At least they weren't stuck up." That would be her younger sister, what was her name, Mary. "You could have a bit of fun with them, here all the kids are indoors as soon as it gets dark. I mean, you're more dead than alive."

"What about you and your husband, Mrs Cameron? You like it, surely? A bit of garden – "

Mrs Cameron folded her arms. "Dad doesn't like it, do you know it's more than ten minutes' walk to the nearest pub. And the garden, don't know what we're going to do about *that*. Haven't got a mower, can't cut the grass."

"What about your neighbours?"

"Them. They wouldn't lend us the dirt from under their nails."

Ocky began to feel his patience ebbing. It was a good thing that Consett had remained in the car. "What do you want, then?"

Mrs Cameron said nothing. Rickie took a formidable-looking knife out of his pocket, pushed the blade in and out. "We want to go home."

Jeannie took up the theme. "Not to those rooms we were in, that was terrible, it was ever so good of you – "

"Oh, Mr Gaye's been *kind*."

"But if perhaps we could get another flat, a bigger one, in our own district. You see, we never thought we should be leaving there altogether. Something with a little more room, it was very small."

"If you'd never gone blabbing to him this would never have happened," Rickie said. "That's what Dad says."

There seemed to be no point in further conversation. Consett was called in and took photographs of Ocky with his arm round Mrs Cameron and Jeannie, of the twins playing in the garden, and finally a family group. The Camerons, all but Rickie, managed unconvincing smiles. Neighbouring children peered into the garden and called out uncomplimentary things. Rickie went off to fight with them. Mrs Cameron came out to the Rolls.

"You'll see what you can do about getting us away, won't you?" she said.

They drove off. Rickie, breaking off from his fight, shouted after them some no doubt obscene phrase. As they got out of the estate Consett said, "They don't look too pleased. Ask me it must be hell, living in a place like that. I wouldn't swop my couple of rooms in Dalston High Street for it."

They drove back to central London. Ocky dropped Consett off, then went home. Claire greeted him warmly.

"There's one of your fascinating criminal friends here, he says his name is Stewart and that you'll want to see him."

Shivers Stewart was a thin man with bad teeth and a slight stammer, who had been an expert cracksman before his career was ruined by the trembling of his hands caused through the onset of Parkinson's disease. He had then become a fence, but after being cut up by a gang which mistakenly thought he had betrayed them to the police, he had abandoned this occupation. His much edited and criminal experiences were to appear in *The Plain Man,* with the implication that he was a totally reformed character, but in fact he was still not above earning a dishonest pound. He was Ocky's most reliable contact with the criminal world.

Stewart was drinking whisky. The glass shook slightly in his hand. Ocky poured some for himself, gave Stewart a cigar.

"Everything's all right," the thin man said. "Reckitts is over in Ireland, he's h-having a regular time of it with his c-cigarettes and a c-couple of women in the house of a friend of mine who's looking after him."

"He was a fine character to pick."

"You w-wanted someone who looked like that picture you showed me. It wasn't easy. I knew he was on the stuff, but I didn't know the way he b-behaved when he got excited."

"What about the girl?"

"She's all right. A friend of mine's taken her away for a month." Stewart sloshed the whisky around in his glass. "I d-don't like it very much. After a murder they're liable to ask questions."

"Will you get it in your head that what happened was nothing to do with Francie Lake, no questions will be asked about it."

"If you say so."

"Just as long as nobody talks before there are any questions."

"I sh-shan't talk," Shivers said almost angrily. Ocky believed him. Shivers Stewart was a professional.

When he had gone, Ocky shouted for Claire. She came in, smiling. They had a couple of drinks to take the criminal taste away, as Ocky put it. He told her about his visit to the Camerons and made it sound purely comic, so that she laughed a lot.

"What will you do?" she asked.

"Try to find them a better flat in the slum they, want to live in, I suppose. It isn't easy to help people. That old business about give 'em a bath and they keep coal in it, there's a lot in that. But we're going to run a campaign – " He told her about the Housing Crusade, and as he talked the idea took on shape and feeling as the ideas in his television programme took on shape and feeling, the force of his personality shone through the ideas, and while he was talking Claire could almost see the cities of the future rising, green and slumless, unfettered by controls yet with all the inhabitants in those millions of family nests swayed by the voice of one benevolent uncle. Those who never met Ocky could never understand, as they often wrote, how honourable people could be so deceived by a cheap crook, failing to understand that those who knew him best saw the crookedness, and saw as they thought beyond it, to some essential unsullied core of true concern for individual human good. So Claire knew that Ocky sometimes slept with other women, as she knew vaguely about his dubious financial operations, and she did not forgive these things so much as she accepted them. She did not think consciously that lechery and crooked dealing were the prices one had to pay for the privilege of possessing a man like Ocky Gaye, it was rather that she accepted the totality of him, lecher and lover, crook and idealist, without wishing in any way to change him. They talked and drank for half an hour. Then he said casually, "By the way, has Dan Deacon telephoned," and she felt the warning flutter in her stomach that told her something was deeply wrong.

"No. Should he have done? I thought he wasn't coming in, that it was all over."

"Not by no means it's not all over." Ocky stared into his glass for a moment, then grinned at her. "If he doesn't ring today he will tomorrow. We've got better fish to fry."

"What fish?" she asked with mock innocence.

Ocky showed her.

Chapter Twenty-Five

Another marble hall, another lift, more corridors, more glass-partitioned cubicles. Quick smelt the air, not so much of wealth as of expense accounts, as he followed a neat girl along the corridors, compared it with the bleakness of New Scotland Yard and thought: *this is the life.* Another door with discreet black lettering: *Miranda Advises. Mary Stead, Women's Post.*

Mary Stead had a brisk air of professional competence. She sat behind a desk that might have been a replica of the one in her husband's office. She removed a pair of bat-eared spectacles, gave him a firm handshake, and looked expectant. Quick felt slightly awkward.

"You'll have read about the death of Miss Lake, early on Wednesday morning." She nodded. "I believe you saw her on Tuesday evening."

"My husband and I were having a drink and she was there, yes."

"You'd never seen her before?"

"No."

"What was your impression of her that evening?"

"Hysterical."

"You wouldn't say she was drunk?"

"If I meant drunk I'd have said it. She was hysterical. Tiresome."

"Now, I believe you left the place where you were drinking on your own. Would you care to tell me about your movements on that evening?"

Mary Stead took out a small gold cigarette-case, offered a cigarette to Quick and took one herself, lighted them both by a gas lighter before he could get a box of matches out of his pocket, puffed smoke and said, "I don't think so. Why?"

He sighed mentally, decided on directness. "Did you know that your husband was carrying on an affair with Miss Lake?"

"I'm not surprised to hear it."

"You're not?"

"Here at *Women's Post*, Sergeant, we're accustomed to dealing with the emotional problems of young married couples. We try to help them in a column called 'Miranda Advises,' which I conduct. You're not married, I can see, so you won't know of my column."

Feebly Quick said, "How do you know? I mean, that I'm not married."

"It's possible to tell," she said cryptically. "The point is this, that it becomes possible to recognise and analyse the defects in one's own marriage as well as in those of other people. Bill unfortunately suffers from an emotional inadequacy that makes him seek the sort of protection and comfort an older woman can offer. I can't give him that kind of thing at all, I prefer complete emotional independence. I don't want to be a pillow for any man's head, but this is basically what Bill requires, as I have often told him. It's the sort of thing an older woman often wants to give. So I am not surprised that Bill should have been carrying on an affair with Francie Lake."

It seemed to Quick that there were flaws in this analysis, but he did not feel capable of pointing them out. "You were on bad terms with your husband?"

"He was often tiresome."

"Did you tell him on Monday evening that you knew he had been going with another woman, and that you were leaving him?"

For the first time she seemed slightly disturbed. She put on the bat-eared spectacles and took them off again. "That gives a wrong idea of the situation, Sergeant. Bill and I are modern, progressive people and I shouldn't have objected to his going with another woman, as you call it, if that had helped us towards an improved relationship. It's no use your saying that it doesn't," she added, although Quick had not been about to say anything. "I can assure you that the problems I face in 'Miranda Advises' are often of this kind, and I always say that complete tolerance is the only answer. However, this does not of course apply when husband and wife have a bad emotional adjustment. It may well be then that a separation is the only answer."

From being too terse she had become altogether too loquacious. Doggedly Quick said, "You did say you were leaving him."

"Yes."

"Yet on the following evening you went round to the *British Volunteer* to meet him."

"Yes. On Tuesday morning Bill was – " She hesitated and Quick feared that she would say "tiresome" but she did not. " – rather insistent that we must discuss things further. I could see little point in it, but I agreed to meet him. We were to go out to dinner and talk things over. In fact, though, I could see that Bill simply wanted a chance to get drunk and become maudlin. I really felt that I'd had enough of all that. I walked out of the pub, went home and packed my things, and stayed the night with my sister. I haven't been in touch with Bill since."

"What was your husband's attitude? Did he want this separation?"

With a slight air of surprise she said, "Why no, he didn't. He simply seemed not to know what he did want. I'm afraid the truth is that Bill is emotionally extremely immature."

When Quick got back to New Scotland Yard, he reported, "She's a corker. Honestly, sir, she shook me, I'd run a mile to get away from a woman like that. Stead didn't know when he was well off."

"That's hardly the point. It seems he didn't want to get away from her. Perhaps she was putting on an act with you, and she was really upset about the affair with Francie Lake."

"You haven't seen her."

"Pity. It destroys that motive we'd thought of for Stead. But still, I think we should go through that alibi of his with a fine tooth comb. Check the places he says he went drinking. Find out if anybody saw him going in or out of this flat, and at what time. And if you find he's said anything, anything at all, out of line, have him in again. And, Quick?"

"Sir?"

"I'll put someone on to checking Mrs Stead's alibi too. You never know, these modern progressive ideas may be a cover for some powerful jealousy."

Quick shook his head. "If she did it, you'll find it was a mercy killing because she thought Francie Lake was too badly adjusted to live."

When Quick rang back an hour later he was distinctly excited. "It looks as if we may be on to something. You know Stead said he went out drinking and got home at about eleven-thirty? Well, I've found a man on the same floor who saw Stead come in at one-thirty in the morning."

"He's sure of the identification?"

"Dead sure. Name's Baswick. He seems to be a pretty snoopy sort of character. Heard a noise in the corridor, thought whoever it was might need help, opened his door and saw Stead going into his own flat. He's sure about the time."

"One-thirty. That would have given him plenty of time to have killed Francie Lake."

"Yes."

"Bring him in again. And if you get a chance to look round his flat, it would help. See if he'll co-operate. It would save issuing a warrant."

"Right." But when Quick rang the bell of Stead's flat there was no answer. A telephone call got no reply. Mary Stead, when Quick rang her up, said she had heard nothing of her husband. And he did not return home that night.

Chapter Twenty-Six

Claud Pyrus, editor of the *Criminal Guide,* had a small bookshop just off Shaftesbury Avenue. In the dusty window there were a number of occult publications and behind them lay stacks of American pulp magazines. In the centre of the window was a glass case containing what appeared to be an embalmed hand. The shop was shut, but there was a bell in the door. Kirton rang this bell. Nothing happened. He rang again.

Above them a window squeaked open. In this dim side street it was possible to see only the shape of a head. A voice said, "Yes?"

"Mr Pyrus?"

"Who wants him?"

"My name is Kirton. I am a subscriber to the *Criminal Guide.*"

"What about it?"

"It's urgent. Connected with a murder."

"A murder." There was, disconcertingly, a horselike whinny above them. "Don't go away. I'm coming down."

By his side Jennifer shivered. "I'm not sure I like this."

"Don't be silly. We've come to ask him a simple question, whether all his copies were sent out at the same time. As soon as we get an answer, we'll go away."

A light came on in the shop, a bolt was drawn back. They entered and found themselves in a room that elaborated the theme suggested in the window. On one wall were books on occult subjects with sections labelled "Levitation," "Histories of Atlantis," "Soul-Currents." Another wall was filled by books on crime, and in unoccupied spaces objects ranging from a dagger to three fragments of a woman's torso reposed in glass cases. Kirton looked at the caption on one of them, and read: "Replica of three pieces of his wife's body, cut up by Doctor Buck Ruxton. The details are all anatomically accurate."

"You are interested in murder?" Mr Pyrus was revealed now as a little man with one shoulder higher than the other, wearing old and rather dirty clothes. As their glances met, Kirton saw that he had quite markedly cross-eyes. One of these eyes now seemed to be staring at him, while the other gazed at Jennifer. "You are interested in murder," Mr Pyrus repeated now more positively. "So am I. I deal in it."

Jennifer yelped sharply. "I'm so sorry. Something brushed my leg. Oh, it's just a cat."

"My familiar." The cat, large and black, jumped on to some books and began to nuzzle Jennifer. She shrank from it. "Don't disturb yourself, my dear young lady, I speak in jest. I call Peterkin my familiar because he is black, but in truth he possesses no supernatural powers. And when I say that I deal in murder, it is only a literary turn of phrase. My murders are on the shelves and in the cases. Here is a fine reconstruction of the unfortunate Violet Kaye, cut up and left in a suitcase in what was called the Brighton Trunk Murder. The blood is rather effective, don't you think? And upstairs I can show you the body of Annie Lawrence, who died of forty-seven stab wounds inflicted by a jealous lover. That is carrying jealousy too far, don't you think? The marks are all beautifully clear." He looked sadly at Jennifer. "The figures are all made of wax, my dear, it is all make believe. But they are made with the most perfect accuracy, and there is a ready market for them. Would you believe it, Mr – I forget your name – "

"Kirton."

"I have had three orders this week for the body of Annie Lawrence. But I am running on. What is your own interest?"

Kirton remembered now that there was a note at the end of each issue of the *Guide*: "Perfect reproductions of weapons and other features of famous criminal cases can be supplied to order." He found that he had to swallow before he could speak. "You've just published a new issue of the *Guide*."

"That is correct."

"Do you work purely on a subscription list? Is the *Guide* on public sale?"

"It is not. I sell a very few copies in the shop here."

"What I want to know is this. When did you post your copies of the last issue? Did you post them all on Monday evening?"

Mr Pyrus kept one eye on Jennifer. The other roamed the room.

"This is all connected with a murder? How delightful, really delightful. You had better come up and tell me about it. And perhaps you will join me in a drink."

"I think if you don't mind," Jennifer said, "I'll just go for a little – "

Mr Pyrus seemed not to hear her. He gripped her arm firmly and guided her up the stairs. Kirton followed. Half-way up it was impossible to avoid seeing Annie Lawrence, stretched full length in her coffin-like case, and illuminated by indirect lighting. The stab wounds were indeed clear. Upstairs there was a small sitting-room, surprisingly neat and extremely warm. Mr Pyrus took three glasses and a bottle from a cupboard. The wine was red, sweet and strong. Kirton could not get it out of his mind that it might be blood.

"You were going to tell me about this case." He put his head to one side. The effect was extraordinary. "Can it be the murder of Miss Lake you are referring to? Don't look surprised. The only other murder during the past few days is a trivial infanticide at Leeds, hardly worth calling murder. Besides, I believe your copy goes to the address of Plain Man Enterprises, doesn't it, Mr Kirton? So you see it is not a remarkable piece of deduction. How did she look?"

"Who?"

"Miss Lake. She was stabbed. Was there much blood?"

"I didn't see the body. Did Miss Lake subscribe to the *Guide*?"

"No. Why?" One roving eye now glared straight at him.

"There was a copy of the new issue in her room."

"How interesting. But anything to do with murder interests me."

"I've gathered that."

Jennifer got up and said decisively, "I'm really not feeling very well. I'll wait outside."

Mr Pyrus chuckled when she had gone. "The young ladies are rather squeamish, it's part of their charm. Where were we now? Ah, yes, I remember. This was an essay in deduction on your part, quite Holmesian one might say. If the *Guide* was posted to its subscribers on Monday night, and if Miss Lake wasn't a subscriber – and she wasn't – somebody must have taken it along and left it there. And since I haven't sold any copies of this particular issue yet in the shop it must have been one of the subscribers. It wasn't your copy by any chance, Mr Kirton?"

"No."

"Just my little joke. You'd hardly be asking if it was, would you? Well now, I think I can help you. But everything in this world costs money, you know. If I have to search my memory, it will cost you something."

"How much?"

"I think we should say five pounds. After all, this is something that nobody knows but me. When I tell you it will make two of us."

They haggled. In the end he gave Pyrus two pounds. The little man put them carefully into his hip pocket.

"I think you'll be pleased with my answer. There are two hundred and fifty subscribers to the *Guide*, and I posted all of the copies myself on Monday evening."

"You're sure of that?"

"As sure as that I'm sitting here." He rubbed his hands together with a sound like the chafing of sticks. "Do you think the police would be interested in this information?"

"I doubt if they'd be much interested. You can pass it on if you like."

"Would you like me to keep it between ourselves? Or do you think it's my duty as a citizen to pass it on?"

"I've told you, do what you like, I don't care." Mr Pyrus insisted on accompanying him downstairs, thrust a damp hand into his. "Goodbye. I've very much enjoyed our chat. I expect you'll be anxious to get back to your young lady. Don't forget, if you ever want to invest in any of my criminal images – it's one of my little jokes, you know, to call them that – you'll know where to come."

Jennifer waited for him on the street corner. "What an awful little man. Do you think he might have killed her himself and left the *Guide* as his trade mark?"

"No." He told her what Pyrus had said about posting the copies.

"That seems to point to Bill Stead, doesn't it? I mean, you know he's a subscriber."

"He could have left it there at some other time, when he took Francie home, for instance."

"But he said he didn't go in."

"Or he could have lent it to her, though that doesn't seem likely. Francie wouldn't have been interested. Or it's possible that Bill has still got his copy of the *Guide*, that would clear him. Are you hungry?"

"No. When I sipped that drink he gave us I thought I was going to be sick."

"Let's have something to take the taste away." They drank hock and ate a sandwich in the Museum Tavern.

"You've been at *The Plain Man* a long time, haven't you?" she asked.

"Eight years."

"Tell me something. If you don't like it, and from the way you talk it seems you don't, why do you stay there?"

"At first I enjoyed it. The whole thing's changed, you know, in the last two or three years, Ocky's changed. It was all quite different when I first went. At least, that's the way I feel. I suppose it could be that I've kidded myself all the time, that I just didn't see through Ocky. I don't know that I've seen through him now."

She nodded her shank of hair. "Daddy had all sorts of doubts about my taking the job, but in the end he said it would be experience. He told me that Mr Gaye – Ocky – was awfully persuasive."

He said abruptly: "Before Elaine died I'd begun to drink quite a lot, but I always thought I could hold it. On this evening I'd had a good deal to drink, Elaine had only had a couple, but I was driving. I turned out of a side road into a main one and ran slap into a lorry. By rights I should have been killed, steering wheel through the chest and so on, but I was just cut and bruised. Elaine hit her head against the dashboard and fractured her skull. When I got her out of the car she was dead. I've never driven a car since."

"I don't see it was a reason for staying."

"I hadn't finished." He got two more glasses of hock. "The first thing I did was to ring Ocky. He told me to say I couldn't remember anything, and wait till he got there. I suppose you could say I was drunk, though I could walk and talk quite well. I ought to have been charged with manslaughter. I wasn't because Ocky bribed the driver of the lorry to say Elaine had been driving. I don't know how much he paid him, but it was enough. The police may have had their suspicions, but there

was nothing they could do. After that, you can see I had to stay."
She said nothing. "For God's sake say something. If I'd been
tried for manslaughter and gone to prison, it wouldn't have
brought Elaine back, wouldn't have helped anyone at all."

"No. I was only thinking – he's a wicked man really, isn't he?
Ocky, I mean. He tried to buy everything."

"I suppose you could say that. He was kind to me
afterwards."

They sat in silence. A simple story, Kirton thought, and
simple to judge it. How could he convey the remorse he had felt,
the nightly sleeping tablets and then, as they were tapered off,
the tears soaking the pillow, the frequent nightmares from
which he woke covered with sweat, the whole pattern of a life
that had lost its small purpose and was now geared wholly to the
needs of Ocky Gaye? Why should she understand it, and if she
did understand why should she sympathise? When she spoke it
was in a tone bright, and even excited.

"I've thought of something. That book about Victorian
journalists that Francie Lake pulled down. I believe there's a
copy of it at home. Shall we go and look?"

"Yes. Though I don't know what there can be to find in it. I
just feel Francie must have had a reason for trying to pull it
down."

The house, off Wilton Place, was tall and narrow. She let
herself in, and said to the woman who appeared through a green
baize door, "Hallo, Mrs Parsons, is my father at home?"

"He is not, Miss Jennifer. I couldn't say when he'll be back."

"We'll be in the library." Jennifer sounded nervous. She
pushed open the door of a room on the right, switched on the
light, and giggled. "Old family retainer type. She terrifies me."

They were in a room of moderate size, with a writing-desk at
one end of it. Around the walls were sets of standard authors,
Wilkie Collins, Charles Lever, Thackeray, Meredith, and also
sets of standard periodicals, among them the *Edinburgh Review*,
Punch, *The Spectator*, *The Contemporary Review*. The effect was

curiously false. Kirton pulled out one volume and assured himself that it was real. Above these rows of formidable volumes, dark-brown portraits looked gloomily down.

"Daddy uses this room when he wants to depress himself. It's very successful."

"I'm not surprised."

"He depresses himself by thinking about the past. Then he cheers himself up by drinking. Shall we cheer ourselves up?" She pointed to a table that held a variety of bottles. "You pour. I'll have whisky and water."

He poured the drinks and they touched glasses. "It's no use thinking about the past," she said. "It's just about the most futile occupation anyone can have."

"I know. Knowing doesn't help much."

"It should do," she said, severely disapproving.

He wandered about the room. "Where do you think this book might be?"

"There are a lot of books of Victorian memoirs and so on over by the door. I thought I'd seen it there."

They found it on the bottom shelf, by the floor, a fat book in a blue binding, *Great Victorian Journalists* by J. Catchment. Kirton flipped through the pages, looked at the contents list, and exclaimed.

"What is it?"

He pointed to one chapter: "The *Pall Mall Gazette* and a Great Victorian Radical."

"Well?"

They were crouched on the floor, and now he thumped it in his excitement. "I should have remembered. The editor of the *Pall Mall Gazette* was W. T. Stead. He wrote some articles to expose the fact that children were sold into prostitution, and got sent to prison."

"For writing the articles?"

"No, no. He bought a young girl and didn't get her father to sign the consent form."

"Bought a young girl?"

"It doesn't matter. You see what Francie was trying to do?"

"Yes. She couldn't manage to write, but she crawled over and pulled out this book with the name in it of the man who killed her."

"That's the way it looks."

"It seems rather an obscure clue."

"Perhaps she meant to open the book and find this chapter and then couldn't manage it. I should have thought of this when I heard the title of the book. Stead was one of the most famous Victorian journalists, and although Francie wasn't a literary type she'd have heard of him."

She said in surprise, "You don't seem as pleased as you ought to be."

"It's too thin. Imagine trying to convince Scotland Yard boys with this sort of stuff. And something else – it's got a smell about it, don't you feel that?" He stopped suddenly.

"What's the matter?"

"That's what Ocky said about the letter, that there was a smell about it, and I think I know why. Bill Stead's an American."

"I don't know what you're talking about." She sat back on her heels in amused exasperation.

He showed her the letter. "Do you see anything queer about the phrasing?" She studied it, and shook her head. He underlined two phrases and two words, *as of now, I want out, gray* and *fender*. "They're all Americanisms, that's why Ocky sensed something was wrong. Francie would never have used them."

"What about '*gray*?' "

"That's an American spelling. No Englishman spells the word that way, we spell it g-r-e-y." He was going on to elaborate when he saw that Jennifer was not looking at, but behind him.

"Daddy." Kirton turned and saw, standing in the doorway, a large bald man with very bushy eyebrows. It was impossible to

149

see the expression of the eyes, but his general mien was not encouraging. It was not, Kirton acknowledged as he scrambled to his feet, perhaps precisely a matter for encouragement when one came in and saw one's daughter sitting on the floor with a man drinking whisky.

"This is Mr Kirton. From the office."

"Ah, yes. You're the young man who told Jennifer to ask questions." The voice was smooth and authoritative.

"Yes. We're making an investigation into Francie Lake's death."

"With the aid of my library. Well, well. Let us all have a drink." In no time, as it seemed, they were sitting in chairs with refilled glasses, and *Great Victorian Journalists* lay neglected on the floor. "I've heard Gaye mention you. Always kindly. You edit one of his papers."

"*Crime Today*, that's right."

"A remarkable man, Ocky Gaye, one of the most remarkable men of our century. He has wonderful gifts. I only wish I could think that he made the best use of them." The eyes in those bush-shrouded caverns remained hidden. "Has your investigation reached any conclusion?"

"Not yet." Boldly he said, "I'm puzzled as to why Francie should come here and ask to look at that paper. A form of guarantee, you said it was."

"I am puzzled, too."

"It wasn't important, Jennifer said."

"The guarantee was routine. There was nothing new about it. As you'll know, Mr Kirton, it is often desirable for a company like Plain Man Enterprises to be controlled by a holding company. Gaye Developments is such a company, and the guarantee is a precautionary measure. It would only operate in the unlikely event of the Plain Man Organisation collapsing. The guarantors are all of the important business men."

"Sir Daniel Deacon?"

"He is one of them. Some of the others are just as – respectable, shall I say? Sir Gravely Wilson, Lord Borboring, Wiley Morecombe, these names mean a good deal in the city, Mr Kirton."

"When Francie Lake brought round the letter you just showed her the guarantee form without question."

"Yes." On the broad mouth there was a twitch of what might be amusement.

"You didn't get in touch with Mr Gaye first."

The twitch was now definitely one of amusement. "No."

"That seems very trusting of you."

"Not at all. Gaye had been in touch with me."

Kirton said to Jennifer. "You didn't tell me that."

"She hadn't been told." Now Masterson looked at Kirton directly. It was as though shutters that had been over his eyes were suddenly raised, and the effect was such as to make Kirton shiver a little. "You are presumptuous, Mr Kirton, even impertinent. I only tell you this now to make sure that you will ask no more questions. Gaye telephoned me to say that Miss Lake, whom he described as one of his most trusted helpers, was worried about the financial position of *The Plain Man*."

"Did he say that she had been thinking of leaving him?"

"No. But I gathered that he wanted to put her mind at rest. He asked me whether I would agree to let her see the guarantee. It was an unusual request, but then Ocky Gaye is an unusual man. I agreed."

"And when she looked at it, did she say anything?"

"She looked at it, she handed it back to me, she said 'Thank you.' Do you like Ocky Gaye, Mr Kirton?"

The question took him by surprise. He found himself almost stammering. "I've worked with him for eight years."

"I ask because I seem to sense a hostility to him which surprises me. I do like him. I like the things he is trying to do, even if I don't always approve of the ways he does them." His hand lightly touched Jennifer's shoulder. "That's why I let

Jennifer work in the Plain Man Organisation." The shutters were down again over the eyes. Kirton found himself gulping out his next words.

"I have one more question."

"I don't promise to answer it."

"Would you say that Gaye Developments makes *The Plain Man* safe, financially? Is it a help to Ocky – Mr Gaye?"

"It is meant to help him. As for safety – I am chairman of Gaye Developments myself. My name means something in the City too, Mr Kirton."

In the hall he said to Jennifer, "I've made a bad impression."

"With Daddy you can never tell. What are you going to do about – the clue in the book, I suppose we ought to call it."

"Think about it and about the letter."

She pressed against him for a moment. The door behind her opened. She said, "Good night."

He walked home through the thin rain, bouncing along the pavements like a man with springs in his heels. In the small sitting-room of his flat he sat down to think about Masterson, about Ocky Gaye, about Bill Stead. Within five minutes his head had fallen on his shoulders. He undressed, got into bed, and fell into a dreamless sleep.

Chapter Twenty-Seven

On the following morning, Friday, Claire came into the bathroom as Ocky was whirling the Indian clubs round his head. She watched him for a few seconds, then began to laugh. He ignored her, continued to rotate the clubs, then rushed to the scales. "Wrong. They're just wrong."

"Oh, darling Ocky," she said. "I do love you."

He stood, tubby in shorts and singlet, shaking his head. "About five pounds wrong."

"You look so funny. Come back to bed."

"I'm late. No time for that."

She rubbed herself against him. "Come on."

"Well, all right."

Afterwards she said, "That girl at the office. Do you do it with her?"

"Mercury? Certainly not. The thought has never entered my head."

"She's pretty. Do you cross your heart – "

"And hope to die. Certainly."

"Nobody else either?"

"Oh, well." Ocky rolled off the bed, put his singlet on again. "You know how it is."

"No, I don't. What do you do?"

"The usual." He pulled on shorts, trousers. "Do you think I'm any thinner?"

"No. But I want to know. I want to *know*, Ocky."

"No time. Besides, it would embarrass you."

"It wouldn't."

"Embarrass me, then." He examined hair, teeth in the glass. "I've got to go. You see what you've done, I shall have no time for breakfast."

"But I want to know. I'm not jealous, Ocky, you can't say I'm jealous."

"I must go."

"Kiss me goodbye." When he went over to the bed she tried to pull him down. "I wish you'd just tell me what you do, that's all. It wouldn't take five minutes."

"No time. See you this evening after the show."

In the car he dictated so fast that Bettridge found it difficult to keep up with him. He entered the Plain Man building like a small whirlwind, scattering beams and nods. He was, after all, a few minutes earlier than usual, and there were no letters on his desk. He rang immediately for Mercury Ellis.

"Post, post, where's the post?" She put the letters on his desk. "What's doing?"

"Mr Crundle's fixed for Mr McClintock to come along at half-past ten to do the filming. He'll come in and have a word with you about it before then." This referred to the opening section of Ocky's programme, showing him in the office, which was always filmed. "I thought you'd want to keep the rest of the morning clear, in case you had to do retakes. A man named Patterson rang last night after you'd gone, very upset because the police had been to see him about some photographs – "

He waved a hand. "Nothing to worry about. Anything more about Francie?"

"Yes. Sergeant Quick rang to know if Mr Stead was here. They've been trying to get hold of him, and apparently he's not at his flat. He hasn't come in yet."

"What's Bill been up to? Dan Deacon hasn't telephoned?"

"No. There is something else, though. A Miss Monterez rang up. She said she'd ring back later."

"I'm not here." The light above one of the desk telephones glowed. Ocky incautiously picked it up.

"Hallo, Ocky. This is Lola."

"Yes?"

"Long time no see." Ocky made no reply to this. "When am I going to see you?"

"Don't know."

"I know you're awfully busy. Your television show's on tonight, isn't it?"

"Yes."

"Wouldn't they be surprised if they knew the sort of thing you got up to in your spare time, Mr Crusader Ocky Gaye?"

Ocky turned over some of the papers on his desk. "What do you mean?"

The Lancashire accent in her voice was very marked. "I'm hard up, Ocky."

In genuine surprise he said, "Why, you silly bitch, are you trying to blackmail me?"

"No need to use hard names. If your telly public knew – "

"Don't be stupid, girl, who would you get to print it?"

"Or your wife."

Ocky began to laugh. Mercury looked at him in astonishment. He laughed so hard that tears came out of his eyes and rolled down his cheeks.

"I don't know what there is to laugh at." Lola sounded offended.

"You do that."

"What?"

"Ring my wife. Tell her I asked you to telephone. Give her all the details. She wants to know." Still laughing, he put down the receiver. "Oh, dear, oh, dear, the things people say, the way they go on."

While he had been talking a light had glowed over another telephone. Mercury was talking on it. Now she put her hand over the mouthpiece. "It's Jack Smedley. He's got Sergeant

Quick in his office looking for Bill Stead. He's not been home all night."

"Out on the tiles, I guess."

"You don't know where he is."

"No idea." He watched her as she put down the telephone and stood waiting. "Is it true that your boyfriend's a boxer?"

"No. As a matter of fact he's an under-manager in Sir Daniel Deacon's firm, the General Building Corporation. I just say that to scare away the wolves."

"Quite right. But you are getting married?"

"Yes."

"Saving for the bottom drawer. You'd better put that in it." He pushed a piece of paper across the desk. She picked it up. It was a cheque for a hundred guineas. Ocky saw with admiration that no emotion touched her elegant features.

"Thank you very much." There was the faint flicker of a smile. "You are in the giving vein today."

Shoulders hunched, head on one side, he orated:

> "Now is the winter of our discontent
> Made summer by this glorious sun and Gaye."

He paused. "Do you know, Mercury, I'm glad I don't come up against you in the way of business."

Chapter Twenty-Eight

"There's a letter from Robert," Bella Deacon said. Robert was at Oxford. "He seems to be awfully much taken up with some film society they've got there. Do you think that's a good thing?"

"I don't know."

"Would you like to read the letter?"

"Not now. Later."

Timidly she said, "What's the matter, Dan? Is it about Ocky Gaye?"

"Yes."

"But there's nothing he can do, I mean do to *us*, is there?" The guilty feeling that was always with her, of enjoying happiness she had done nothing to deserve, seemed to fill her whole body.

As though he were interpreting these thoughts her husband said, "I've made you happy, Bella, haven't I?"

"Oh, yes." She stretched out a plump hand. "Happier than I deserved, Dan."

"It's been better than you expected, hasn't it, when you married me?"

"I don't know what I expected. You know I've always looked up to you and so have the boys. It's been wonderful." He patted her hand. "I can't bear the thought that anything might take it away."

"Bella, I want you to listen to what I'm going to say. There's an image of me that you've built up in your mind. I don't say it's

157

untrue, but it's only part of the truth. We're all of us three or four people, and you only know one. Do you understand?"

"No." She almost cried out the word. She meant, he knew, that she did not want to understand. "I've got faith in you, Dan. I know you'd never do anything wrong."

"If I had – if it could be made to appear that I'd done – "

"Oh, but it couldn't," she said with perfect confidence. Timidly, she added, "You're too proud, Dan. If it's a matter of – well – paying off Ocky Gaye, why don't you do that and get rid of him."

"It's not that simple. I don't know that it would get rid of him. And anyway, there are some things you can't do." He rose from his chair.

"You haven't eaten your breakfast." She said it with dismay. Emotional disturbances had never disturbed her own capacity for eating large meals and even now she was torn between the wish to comfort him and the awareness that a mound of scrambled egg was cooling on her plate.

He came round the table, kissed the top of her head, and left the house. She watched him walking along the road, treading what might have been a private tight rope along the pavement. At the end of the street he turned, raised his bowler hat and waved. She waved back. Then she ate her scrambled egg while she reread Robert's letter.

Sir Daniel Deacon read and commented on his post in a manner that satisfied Miss Brocklebank that he was really back to his old form. The only thing that seemed to her slightly odd was that he asked twice whether a man named Deverston had been in touch, and asked particularly that he should be put through immediately if he telephoned. Miss Brocklebank, who prided herself on her efficiency, needed to be told such things only once. When the man did ring up, she put him through and going into Sir Daniel's office when the call was over, she found him smiling. It had been good news, then, and, a faithful satellite, she smiled responsively back at him.

Five minutes later he spoke to Ocky Gaye on the telephone.

"Gaye," he said. "Deacon. It won't wash. You made a mistake."

Ocky's voice was warm, rich, untroubled. "What?"

"You mentioned a hotel near Paddington. I've been able to trace it. The Eugene Hotel, right? The man I employed has talked to the manager and the clerk and he's put the fear of God into them. They don't want to be brought into a case that's going to court. They're not going to swear to anything at all." Deacon's voice was raised a little, exultantly. "Your whole tinpot scheme is done for, Gaye, do you understand?"

"You've been suborning witnesses, is that right? It's a serious thing to have done."

Deacon barked with angry laughter. "You wouldn't dare to put those men into a witness-box."

"I don't suppose they would want to give evidence, no."

He could not resist savouring his triumph. "I want you to understand, Gaye, that if I ever hear from you again – "

"There is still the matter of Gwyneth." Ocky's voice was sad. "I'm sorry you drive me to it, Dan."

"What do you mean?"

"It's a story we could splash in *The Plain Man*. An interesting sidelight on the youth of a famous personality. We could do it in a way that kept clear of libel. We wouldn't draw any conclusions, of course, we'd leave our readers to do that, just report the facts. Facts are sacred, isn't that so? And Bella doesn't know the facts, does she, they'll be news to her." Deacon stared straight in front of him, listening to the persuasive voice. "I don't want to have to do this, Dan, I hate to do it. You're forcing my hand. You must come in, do you understand that?" There was silence. The voice went on. "I wouldn't use – "

Deacon put down the receiver. He looked across the room, at a particular patch of oak panelling. He thought about Bella as he had seen her first, wonderfully girlish and gay, and then about the woman he had left at the breakfast table that morning, wrapped in her cocoon of happiness. The telephone on his desk rang three times before he answered it.

"I have Mr Gaye on the line."

"Tell him I do not wish to speak to him. Tell him in those exact words."

"Yes, Sir Daniel."

He opened a drawer in his desk and took out the revolver which he had bought years ago after a burglary had taken place in the building. He looked at its solid hostile blueness. He put it down hurriedly on the desk and covered it with some papers, as Miss Brocklebank tapped on the door and came in.

"I just wanted the Fawkes file, Sir Daniel." She stared at him. "Are you feeling well?"

"Perfectly well, thank you. Here are the papers."

"Isn't there something I can get you, some – some indigestion tablets?"

"Nothing whatever." With less asperity, smiling even, he said, "You've looked after me wonderfully well, Miss Brocklebank. Thank you."

She went out, dazzled by the smile and began to type in the adjoining office. She stopped typing as it struck her that there had been something odd about the form of Sir Daniel's last words. Then she heard the shot. She opened the door of his office, stared for a moment unbelievingly at what she saw, and then began to scream.

Chapter Twenty-Nine

Kirton got out of bed, bathed, washed and shaved. In the bath he found himself singing, something he had not done for years. Slapping on after-shave lotion he contemplated his face in the mirror, the thick hair neatly brushed, the face still round and boyish, the teeth – he opened his mouth – still good. Under the eyes were dark shadows which had not yet become pouches, marks that exercise and a reduction in drinking would cure. He envisaged brisk twenty-mile walks through the countryside, ending with beer in a rustic pub. Then he looked out of the bathroom window, saw that it was spitting with rain, burst out laughing, and addressed the face in the glass: "Charles Kirton, you're being extremely corny."

He dressed with particular care, putting on a gay spotted tie. When he pushed open the door of the *Crime Today* office he was whistling. He stopped when he saw Jack Smedley sitting at one of the desks, looking unusually solemn. In a chair, also looking solemn, was Sergeant Quick. Before he could speak, Smedley said, "The sergeant wants to see Bill Stead. Apparently he hasn't been home all night, and he hasn't turned up here this morning."

Kirton looked at his watch. "It's early yet. I'd like to see Bill myself, for the matter of that. Probably he's been staying with friends."

"Perhaps," Quick said noncommittally.

"Have you asked Ocky?"

"Mr Smedley has kindly spoken to Mr Gaye and he had no idea where Mr Stead was. Mr Gaye is a busy man, I wouldn't want to worry him." In a hushed voice Quick said, "He'll be preparing for his TV show tonight, I expect."

"Probably. Well, I don't see what we can do but wait. Did you want Bill urgently?"

"We believe he can help us with our inquiries. You said you wanted to see him also, Mr Kirton. Would that be in connection with your own investigation?"

"It might be, yes. Could we swop stories, do you think?"

"You know I couldn't possibly do anything like that, sir. And I must remind you that it is your duty to give any information you have obtained to the authorities."

What had they got to lose by telling the police? Nothing, Kirton decided. He took Quick into his little cubicle and told him of the American phrases in the letter, about the *Criminal Guide* and about the name of Stead occurring in the book about Victorian journalists. Quick did not seem greatly impressed.

"Very literary, most of that, wouldn't you say? I respect literature in its proper place, mind. But you couldn't hope to convince a jury with that sort of stuff, could you now? I mean perhaps Miss Lake had slipped into the habit of using American phrases now and then, wouldn't you think that was possible?"

"Since you ask me, no. I've never heard her use such phrases, or spell the word grey with an 'a.'"

"And then this paper you're talking about, the *Criminal Guide,* there doesn't seem to be much in that. Stead might say he'd given his copy of it to Miss Lake here in the office."

"What for? She had no interest in that sort of stuff."

"So your conclusion is that Stead must have been in Miss Lake's flat last night, although he denied it?"

"It looks rather that way to me."

"Since you've been frank with me," Quick said rather ponderously, "I don't mind telling you that we've reached much the same conclusion. That's why we'd like to talk to him."

The telephone rang. Mercury said, "Can you go into Mr Gaye's office? It's about tonight's programme."

He made his excuses to Quick. "I absolutely understand," the sergeant said. "Please tell Mr Gaye that we shall interfere as little as we possibly can with your operations. It's a privilege to see the way that you gentlemen work."

The cameras had been set up in Ocky's room.

Jimmy Crundle was pacing up and down talking, the sweat running off him. He was arguing with the producer, Alex McClintock, a long-nosed young man with dandruff on his shoulders. Ocky sat behind his big desk looking bored, as he was always bored by technical discussion.

Jimmy was in mid-flight. "It's about the way the programme should go tonight, Boy. This is the way I see it. First we have Ocky talking about Francie, telling the story, what she was like, right-hand woman and all that. Then he says Plain Man Enterprises are all out to help the police, put their special Crime Bureau on to it. Wham – on to the Crime Bureau with you, Boy, coming in to see Ocky."

McClintock shook his head. "Too much talk. We cut to Kirton in his office, starting the investigation. Then go on to show what he's been doing."

His voice held an interrogative note. Jimmy said, "Can we show that, Boy? What have you been doing?" Ocky took out his gold toothpick and began to use it. Kirton said nothing. "Would it be better to move to Bill Stead, last person to see Francie and all that, dropped her outside the flat."

"Bill's not around." Kirton paused and said without emphasis, "The police are getting a warrant to search his flat."

Jimmy pursed his lips and let out breath like a steam engine. McClintock looked down his long nose. Ocky went on picking his teeth. "We'd better leave Bill out of it, then." Without waiting for comment, Jimmy went on, "A quick look at Francie's office and then we'll have somebody, doesn't matter who it is, who was in the pub with her that Tuesday evening, same old Francie, went off home as usual. Plot her journey home, animated map if you like. Then our team of investigators asking questions round about, can do, Boy?" Kirton nodded. "Let's lay that on for this afternoon, okay, Alex? All right. Cut back to our office, co-ordinating results and that cock, we shall need you for that, Boy, and Jack too. Bring in Ray Pillin to say how he took the pictures along the night before, discovered her body on Wednesday morning."

"Leave Ray out of it." That was Ocky from the desk.

"But Chief, he was the last person to see her alive, he found her body."

"I said, leave him out of it. Leave the pictures out. We don't want that part of the story."

Jimmy looked at Ocky. "Okay. Then we have the last section, the one with real punch, the Chief and Boy here discussing the case in Francie's flat, going into all the details, going over the evidence. Wind up with the chief asking: 'Who killed Francie Lake? Do you know anything. Can *you* help.'"

McClintock ran a hand through his sandy hair. A few flakes of dandruff floated down. "Thin."

Jimmy spread expressive hands. "What do you want? It's got everything."

"No climax. You don't lead up to anything. You need – I don't know – a suspect, or some question which Mr Gaye can ask at the end." He ticked the questions off on his fingers. "What was the meaning of the mysterious letter found in the typewriter? Why were there three different brands of cigarettes in the ash-tray, only one smudged with lipstick? And so on."

"But there weren't any cigarettes."

"I know that," McClintock said irritably. "I'm just telling you the sort of question."

"Perhaps I can help." Kirton told them of his discoveries. Ocky put down his toothpick and listened. When he had finished there was silence. Then Jimmy wiped his forehead and spoke.

"Doesn't look good for Bill. I knew he was having an affair – "

Ocky asked: "With Francie?"

"Yes. But I didn't suppose either of them took it seriously."

"What do we do?" That was McClintock. All of them were looking at Ocky, who put down the toothpick.

"I'm not going to throw Bill to the wolves. But we can do this without mentioning names. The letter Francie left, for instance, Boy and I agree that she didn't write it, because of the American turns of phrase, but we don't go any further. Same with the *Criminal Guide*. We point out that it was posted on Monday night, reached subscribers Tuesday morning. We ask: who are the subscribers? And over the book Francie pulled down we simply ask: What does this mean, why did she do it? All right?"

"Terrific," Jimmy said. "We're putting out leads for the police to follow if they feel like it. We're not pointing a finger at anybody. Just the same, I wonder where Bill's got to."

McClintock was looking at his watch. The light glowed on Ocky's desk. He frowned, picked up a receiver. Mercury Ellis' voice, for once a little uncertain, said: "Sorry to disturb you. You know I told you my fiancé worked in the General Building Corporation? He's just rung me through with some news. I thought you ought to know it."

"Yes?"

"Sir Daniel Deacon shot himself in his office this morning. He's dead." Ocky said nothing for a few seconds. He was looking straight at the John portrait. "Did you get that?"

"Yes. You're a good girl, Mercury. Thank you very much." He replaced the receiver, put his hands on the desk palm downwards, bowed his head. His pale face was suffused with a deep blush.

McClintock shifted his feet. "We're working to a tight schedule. Can we go on?"

Ocky looked up. Slowly the colour faded from his face. "I've just heard some very bad news. Sir Daniel Deacon, an old friend, has died in his office. This morning, not more than an hour or two ago. It's a shock. Just give me ten minutes, Alex, will you?" The three of them moved towards the door. "Not you, Boy. I'd like to talk to you."

When they were alone Ocky said, "This is a terrible thing, Boy. He shot himself."

"Why?"

"Because he couldn't bear to have the past revealed. That story you found out about him in Wales, every word of it was true. That's why he shot himself."

"You were blackmailing him."

"Look at it the right way, Boy. All I wanted was for Dan to come in with us. It was what Deacon knew about his motives that made him kill himself."

"You were blackmailing him and I helped you to do it."

Ocky got up, came round the desk, put a hand on his shoulder. For the first time in his life he shook off the hand.

"You're being soft and taking it hard. That's a bad combination, Boy. You know I wouldn't have done this unless I'd been driven to it. I don't like it any more than you do. More than that, it's a real disaster for me. I'd relied on Dan coming in. But you don't see me crying."

"Why are you telling me this?"

"I don't want you to get any wrong ideas. You might be thinking of talking to the police about Dan. If you did, you'd be admitting that you got the information about him yourself, you'd be in it right down deep. And I doubt if they'd be interested, anyway. It's got no connection with Francie."

"What has got a connection with Francie? Why did you send her round to Masterson's house with that letter?"

Ocky's answer was ready. "She kept pestering me, saying we were on the skids, had no firm backing behind us since Jimmy Jeavons died. I told her there were people who had enough faith in me to guarantee *The Plain Man* up to half a million. She refused to believe it, and she was getting hysterical, so I told her she could see the guarantee. I rang up Masterson, and sent her round to him with a letter."

"And was she satisfied?"

"I don't know about that and I don't much care. What's on your mind, Boy?"

"I'm not sure."

"Do you really think a man like Masterson would let himself be connected as chairman with something that wasn't straight?"

"Deacon was one of the guarantors."

"That's right. And the others were the same calibre. There are still some people who've got faith in Ocky Gaye."

Kirton crossed to the great window and looked down on to the tiny people below. He felt strongly, as he had not felt for years, a sense of identification with those people, a wish to be part of them and not, as one was from this vantage point, remote from their lives. Ocky had uncanny skill in interpreting such thoughts.

"We're not like them, you know, we can't be. Our lives are bound to be imperfect. What are those lines by – is it Yeats?

> A man has power to choose
> Perfection of the life or of the work.

Something like that. You can't have both."

"The work. That's really a joke." He turned from the window. "If I'm to keep my mouth shut, I want to know what it's all about. I'm supposed to be an investigator, let me investigate. Where's Ray Pillin?"

"The police have talked to him. They're satisfied." Ocky was mildly reasonable. "I seem to remember a deputation that came along once to tell me Ray did the organisation no credit. Where something like this is concerned I'm agreeing with them, that's all. I gave him a bonus and told him to keep out of the way. We don't want our brand image tarnished now, do we?"

"Let me talk to him."

Ocky shook his head. "Sorry."

He started to say something, then went out. He went two floors down to the Accounts Department, and talked to Paula Layne, a girl he had taken out once or twice in the past.

"Paula, the Chief wants me to get in touch with Ray Pillin about a bonus he's had, and he can't find the address. Ray's under cover for the moment." He closed an eye. "Can you get it for me?"

"It's not strictly kosher, but seeing that it's you…" She went away and came back with an address written down on a piece of paper. "You're a stranger lately."

No reply to this seemed possible. Kirton kissed her on the cheek.

Chapter Thirty

Quick talked to Nevers on the telephone and told him of Kirton's discoveries and theories. To his surprise the superintendent seemed impressed. He had just put down the receiver when Jack Smedley said, "Call from reception. Bill Stead's on his way up in the lift."

Quick was waiting when the lift discharged Stead, pale-faced, with a cut over one eyebrow and a bruised cheek. They walked together to Stead's office. Inside it the sergeant said, "Do you mind telling me where you were last night, Mr Stead?"

"I don't see it's your business, but I don't mind telling you. I took a girl I know to a theatre, then to a night club, got mixed up in a fight there and then – "

"Yes?"

"I went home with her and stayed the night."

"You'll be able to provide confirmation of this story, sir, no doubt."

"I suppose so, if it's really necessary."

"But that's not the chief purpose of my visit. Are you a subscriber to a publication called the *Criminal Guide*?"

"Yes, I am. But what's this got to do with anything?"

"Did you receive the latest issue of the *Guide* on Tuesday morning?"

"I dare say, yes. I brought it to the office."

"Have you got it here now?"

"I expect so. What *is* all this about?"

"Would you mind looking for it?"

Stead looked on his desk and in its drawers. "I can't seem to find it. It may have been thrown away."

"Shall we ask your secretary, or would you agree that you took it along and left it at Miss Lake's flat on Tuesday evening? That's where it was found."

"I don't remember." Stead's finger went to the bruise on his cheek. "I told you, I never went in."

"I should like you to accompany me to New Scotland Yard," Quick said formally.

It was half-past three in the afternoon when Stead had finished making the addition to his original statement. It was read back to him, while Nevers and Quick listened.

"… I wish to make the following addition to my statement of Thursday, 13 October. In my original statement I said that I left Frances Lake at about eight-thirty in the evening, and did not see her again or return to her flat. I now wish to amend this. After I left her I went home, as I said before and discovered that my wife was not there. I went out drinking in several pubs, but I did not return home as I said, at eleven-thirty. Instead I went to see Frances Lake. I cannot say exactly why I did so, except that I blamed her for the strained situation between my wife and myself, and had the feeling that I might be able to settle something by seeing her. I was rather drunk at the time. I got to her flat between eleven-thirty and midnight. She was still dressed and at first seemed pleased to see me, but later we quarrelled. She said that I should never be happy with my wife and advised me to leave her. She repeated again that if Mary would give me a divorce we could get married. I asked if she didn't think that Mr Gaye would object. She took offence at this and said that he had no control over her actions. We quarrelled about this, and I left the flat. I did not strike her. When I left she was fully dressed. I should think that I left the flat just before one o'clock, and I walked home. I do not know exactly what time I arrived home, but I was seen by a neighbour as I went in.

"With regard to the copy of the *Criminal Guide* found in the flat, I accept that this is my copy and that I received it on Tuesday morning, but I am sure that I did not take it to the flat myself, and I have no idea how it got there. I know nothing at all about the letter found in the typewriter."

Stead signed the statement and looked expectantly at Nevers.

"You are sure you have nothing to add to that statement."

"No. I've told you the truth."

When Stead had been taken outside the superintendent jabbed with a pencil on the blotting pad in front of him. At last the sergeant said, "Do we hold him, sir?"

"No." In face of Quick's mute rebelliousness the superintendent explained. "As you said yourself, it's thin, there's not enough to put to a jury. I follow young Kirton's reasoning, I think he's been clever and very likely he's right, but we've got to have a great deal more than a clever piece of reasoning. I've got something else in mind, though. This TV show of Gaye's may be useful."

"How?"

"In building up pressure on Stead." Nevers' smile was grim. "If I know Gaye he'll find a way of bringing in this stuff that Kirton's discovered. I shouldn't be surprised to learn if Stead did something – silly, shall we say? – as a result of that telecast."

"To tell you the truth, sir, I thought you might want to stop Gaye's show."

"If I thought it necessary I would, for all his friends in high places. But I think he may help us."

"And in the meantime we let Stead go." Quick still sounded doubtful.

"For the moment. But we keep a fatherly eye on him."

171

Chapter Thirty-One

It was half-past two before Kirton was able to get away from the office. He ate sandwiches in a snack bar, and then went back for a programme conference. Dex, buzzing with rumour, was waiting for him with Jack Smedley and Alex McClintock.

"You know Bill's gone off with that sergeant. What do you suppose it's all about?"

"You'd better ask him."

"But you were talking to the sergeant. He must have told you something."

"He said he thought the superintendent was getting a warrant to search Bill's flat."

Dex pulled at his lower lip. "This might help the paper circulationwise. We'd defend him, of course. Can't you see the headlines. Not that I want it to happen."

"Of course not."

"What about tonight?" Smedley asked. "Shall we have to hold up the programme if Bill's arrested? Is there any point in going ahead with that door-to-door stuff we had set for this afternoon?"

"I believe we ought to go ahead," McClintock said. "If Scotland Yard make us scrap the thing at the last moment, we'll have to do that. But I'd like to take some film as soon as we've done with Ocky, Boy, showing you talking to Jack here about the form of the investigation. I don't think we want the other researchers in on it, just the two of you talking about the way it should be handled. You can talk about putting the machinery in motion, plotting her journey home, getting the investigators to work, okay? Can you two mug up a sort of script and run through it together? We want it extemporaneous sounding, but fluent, mind you. Three to four minutes, no more. Then we end up with Smedley beginning to brief the researchers and cut to them on the job."

"I suppose I ought to be going," Dex said unwillingly. "Keep in touch, Boy."

"I'll do that."

McClintock went off to see how Ocky, who hardly needed the help of a producer, was getting on. Kirton and Smedley settled down to plan their scene. The form of what they were doing was not new to them, although the subject matter was. They had settled on words and movements when McClintock came back, twenty minutes later. The setting up and shooting of the scene took over an hour.

The address he had got from Paula was a back street in Bow. He climbed uncarpeted stairs, past cooking smells and the sound of foreign voices. A paint-peeled door on the top floor bore the name "Pillin" in a surprisingly elegant script. He knocked. The door opened a little and Ray Pillin's head peeped out like a rat's from a hole. He stared at Kirton.

"I've come with a message." The photographer said nothing but opened the door wider. He went in.

The room had a skylight, but no window. The bed, unmade, was in one corner. Some dirty carpet covered most of the floor.

"This room needs a woman's hand," Kirton said lightly. On the table was some old newspaper, out of which Ray had been eating fish and chips. The room smelt of food, of urine, of Pillin who stood, toes turned inwards, rat-eyes suspicious. In one corner the door to a kitchenette was open, and revealed piled-up plates.

Pillin sat down at the table and screwed up the fish and chip paper. "You come from the chief?"

"That's right. Why do you live in a place like this, Ray, when you don't have to?"

"Suits me, see. I don't have to explain to you why I live here, do I?"

"Of course you don't."

"Well, then." The little eyes looked hard at him. "What d'you want?"

"You've got a story to tell."

"Don't know what you mean. I've told it."

There was something queer about Pillin, he thought, and then realised what it was. The photographer's usual obsequiousness had been replaced by a manner almost belligerent.

"You've told a story, yes. But you and I know it's not the real one. I'm investigating Francie's death for Ocky, the chief, you know that. He wanted you to tell me the real story."

"Pity he didn't say so." Pillin was still screwing up the fish and chip paper, his elegant small hands with their dirty nails bunching it up. Kirton saw plain paper among the newsprint.

"Let's have a look, Ray."

"What?"

"The paper." He made a gesture across the table. Pillin threw the paper across the room as if it had become red-hot, half rose. The paper was beside the bed. Kirton walked across, bent to pick it up. Pillin's voice, sharp, said: "Don't do that."

He looked up and saw, with astonishment, a revolver held in the photographer's fist. In a small but steady voice Pillin said, "Don't pick it up. I don't want you here."

Genuinely surprised, he said, "Ray, you're being ridiculous. Put that away."

"I've answered all the questions I'm going to. I'm not talking any more."

"But Ocky himself sent me here. How else would I know where you were?"

"I don't care. Get out."

"All right."

He walked towards the door and then when he had reached the table, pushed it over at Pillin and dived sideways. The photographer had been standing close to the table. One edge of it hit him on the arm and knocked the revolver from his hand. It fell with a clatter to the floor. Kirton reached it first. "Now, then," he said, and pointed the revolver at Pillin.

"It's not loaded," Pillin was edging across the room towards the paper. Kirton moved over, picked it up, unscrewed it. He read, in Ocky's distinctive hand: "Boy has been asking questions. In case he contacts you, you know the story."

"So you were expecting me." Pillin did not answer. "What does this mean, you *know the story*."

"Means what it says. You know it too."

"What story. What is the story? Why did Ocky send this note?"

"You'd better ask him."

"I'm asking you." Kirton broke open the revolver. It was unloaded. "What does it mean? You took some other photographs along, didn't you?"

He stepped forward. Pillin stepped back. The room was too small and bare for much manœuvring and Pillin was driven into a corner. He prepared himself for a spring, but when Pillin's movement came he was unready. He had expected an attack, but the little man darted not forward but sideways, under his outstretched arm and towards the door. Kirton turned and, with a vague recollection of the rugger tackles which he had suffered and disliked in youth, dived. More by luck than skill he caught one of Pillin's legs and brought him down. Then they rolled together, struggling ridiculously on the dirty carpet. But the struggle did not last long. Kirton, no athlete, was yet much the stronger of the two. He seized Pillin's head and banged it again and again on the floor. As he did so a kind of passion took possession of him. I could kill this dirty little bag of bones, he thought, I could easily kill him. He put his hands round the scrawny throat, squeezed. Pillin's face reddened, his eyes popped out, he made strangled sounds, beat feebly with his legs. He could do nothing with his arms, which were pinioned by Kirton's knees. Holding on to the throat, feeling it writhing under his hands, Kirton thought quite impersonally: *I believe I'm going to kill him.* Then suddenly he let go. The flood of feeling that came pounding in on him was composed partly of horror at the act he had almost committed, partly of disgust at the smell of the creature still pinned beneath him. Behind this, reaching back into the past, there was the recollection of some occasion at school when a boy had knelt on him in just this way, pinning arms to ground, squeezing throat. He remembered his fear, the look of pleasure on the boy's face. Shuddering, he moved off Pillin.

"You nearly croaked me." The little man sat up on the floor, stroking his throat, looking at Kirton with wonder and terror.

"Next time I might." He spoke threateningly, but he knew that there would be no next time, that he could hardly bear to touch Pillin. Looking at the quivering thing on the floor, though, he saw that the battle was already won. "You took some other photographs. Tell me about them."

"You'll have to take the can back. I'll tell the chief you made me tell you."

"That's right. You tell him that."

"There was a man and a girl. They went into a hotel and the girl was to scream and then I was to take pix of them together, you know. But it went wrong, the man was high on tea, and he went for the girl."

"Those were the pictures you took to Francie."

"Prints and negs, that's right."

"Who were they, the man and the girl?"

"Don't know. I didn't have anything to do with it except just taking the pix. I can tell you one thing the chief said, though. 'We're not using it,' he said. 'There won't be any publicity.' "

"I don't understand."

"Nor me. But I don't try." His glance was venomous, he still rubbed his throat.

"What did they look like?"

"He was a city gent type, bowler and umbrella, you know. Grey hair. Sharp face, good looking I suppose you'd call him, about fifty-five. The girl was just a little tart. Very young."

"Very young?" Kirton began to understand. "Would you say she was sixteen?"

"Might not have been. She looked like a schoolgirl, only tarted up."

"Did the man look anything like this?" He drew out a pencil and on the back of Ocky's note, sketched Deacon.

Pillin considered it critically. "A bit, yes. Mind you, you haven't got the way he looks really."

"I don't suppose I have. And you don't know who it was?"

The little man shrugged. "Why should I care? I do what I'm told."

It was true. Pillin would do without question whatever Ocky told him to do. "One more question. What was the hotel?"

Pillin looked rebellious for a moment, then named it.

Chapter Thirty-Two

When the filming session was over, Ocky ate a turkey sandwich and drank half a bottle of Pol Roget. Then he sent for Jimmy Crundle.

"Jimmy, what about the Camerons?"

"The Camerons? Oh, yes, the Camerons." Jimmy wiped his forehead. "I've had a hell of a lot on my plate today, we've got this show tonight, a ticklish one, and – "

"You've done nothing, is that the answer?"

"I've got some inquiries in line. It's a hell of a district where they lived, pretty near to impossible to get anything decent. Why they want to move out of the place they're in I don't know. I looked at it myself. A wonderful kitchen unit, as neat a little fridge as I've seen."

"You're talking like an advertisement for the Ideal Homes Exhibition. We're dealing with people, not kitchen units, and people don't like being dragged away from their homes. We should have understood that. Did you get in touch with Mr Emanuel?"

"The landlord, yes, but he wanted two thousand, and it's a short lease."

"What's it worth?"

In his confusion Jimmy almost stammered. "I don't know, it's hard to say because of the profit he makes out of it, hell of a profit, but of course the proper value is nothing like that, in fact the place should really be condemned."

"It was a home for the Camerons, and it's going to be their home again. The whole house, mind you, not seven people in two rooms."

"No good, even if you buy the house you won't be able to get the other tenants out, or at least it will be the hell of a job."

"Oh." Ocky was sometimes surprisingly ignorant of the facts of life. He asked quietly, "What do you suggest?"

The quietness, Jimmy knew, was dangerous. It was an occasion for using the respectful *Chief* rather than the familiar *Ocky*. "As a matter of fact I had my secretary ring all the local estate agents and there's a flat in the next street that's vacant. It's four rooms and a kitchen, share bathroom, but they want five hundred premium for it, daylight robbery. I haven't seen the place, but it won't be a patch on the little house we've put them in, and it's not big enough really."

"Why didn't you tell me this before? Get on to this estate agent now, fix things with him, offer him three hundred premium, he'll jump at it. Tell him the Camerons want to move in today, you understand that, today. Then get down there and set about organising a welcome home party. I want flags waving, people cheering, glad to see them back. One of the boys belongs to a street gang called the Arabs, get them to rally round. Put some furniture in the flat, if they haven't got any there. I want to fix it so that the Camerons are back home by six o'clock tonight." Jimmy's mouth was wide open. "You'll have to send somebody down to tell them about it, but you won't have any trouble, they're mad to come back."

"It's impossible, Chief, impossible." Jimmy was almost weeping. "I've got a TV programme to look after."

"Get someone else to do it. What are you doing anyway, but stooging round after McClintock. He doesn't need you."

"But we shan't even be able to get the agreement signed today."

"Who said anything about signing agreements? Money talks, Jimmy, nothing louder. Don't make me feel too sorry that

Francie's gone." Ocky got up from behind the desk. His voice was agreeable enough, but Jimmy felt as though cold water were running down his back. "I want to help the Camerons, you understand? I want them back in their own district, where they like to be, and I'm going to be there to greet them. Then next week we have Jeannie back on the programme, telling the whole story. Think you can do it?"

Jimmy did not dare to say no.

Ocky telephoned Bella Deacon, but was told that she was prostrated by shock. He left a message of sympathy. When Nevers rang he expected to hear of Stead's arrest, but the superintendent merely said that Stead had been very helpful to them in answering some more questions.

"He remembered one or two things he'd forgotten the first time, if you take my meaning, Mr Gaye."

"And you're quite satisfied he's in the clear now? I'm delighted to hear it. Young Bill's a good lad."

"Let's say we're satisfied for the moment, shall we, sir? I wanted to have a word about your television programme tonight. Your producer has given me an outline of the approach you're making. I wanted to let you know that I've no objection to it. You understand that no comment must be made on any individual."

"Of course we do. What are you getting at, Superintendent?"

"I hope you understand me, Mr Gaye, when I say that I've got no objection, in these rather exceptional circumstances, to your unorthodox approach." Nevers chuckled unexpectedly. "In fact, you may even find yourself assisting the course of justice. I'm sure you'll enjoy the experience."

After the telephone call from Nevers Ocky stared thoughtfully at the John portrait, then called Mercury Ellis in and began dictation. He was interrupted by a call from Ray Pillin. He listened to what the photographer had to say, speaking mostly in monosyllables himself, then got up and went over to the big window. He remained there so long that Mercury coughed. Ocky turned round, smiling.

"Mercury, my dear, I hadn't forgotten you were there."

"Bad news?"

"Not exactly. Someone trying to be clever and being silly, that's all. Someone who should know better."

He resumed dictation, but was interrupted by two more telephone calls. The first was from Jimmy Crundle, to say that all the arrangements were under way for restoring the Camerons to their native slum, and that they should arrive there by half-past five. Jimmy was triumphant, and Ocky allowed his voice to become meltingly warm as they talked. The second call was from Shivers Stewart.

"I see Deacon's c-croaked himself. I don't like it. What's going to happen?"

Ocky was laconic. "Nothing."

"This nark he had making inquiries at the hotel put the f-fear of God into Matvos, that's the manager. I don't like it."

"Do you think I do? It's unfortunate, man, but nothing is going to happen."

"If the coppers find out what you were trying to do to him – "

"Who's going to tell them? Your boy and girl, they're all right?"

"I to-told you, that end's all sewn up. It was a job."

"Then we've got nothing to worry about."

After he had put down the telephone, however, Ocky had the disturbing sense of a world crumbling before his eyes – or, better, a more personal image, he was the captain on the bridge of a sinking ship, issuing orders to stop one leak and then another, only to find that half a dozen more had appeared in different parts of the vessel. He touched the Epstein head for reassurance, fingers passing over the absolute solidity of bronze hair, poking in eye sockets, stroking nose. Then he crossed to the big window, looked down. "The captain goes down with his ship." He clicked heels together, saluted.

"Whatever are you doing?"

He turned, saw Mercury staring at him, burst out laughing. "Practising my recitation of 'The boy stood on the burning deck.' "

"I don't understand."

"That's always been my trouble. Nobody understands me."

"I didn't thank you properly for that cheque. It was very kind." He saw with surprise that Mercury was embarrassed, waved his hand. "And Jimmy's been on again. Everything's laid on for you to welcome the Camerons back, and you ought to get moving. McClintock wants you and Kirton at Francie Lake's flat by seven o'clock."

"Yes. You'd better come too, Mercury, just to look after things."

They went down in the Rolls and on the way Ocky talked to her about the politicians he had known, the giants of a past that seemed to her unimaginably distant, Cripps and Bevin, Churchill and Waverley, Morrison and Attlee. In these stories Ocky himself played the inconsiderable part of a terrier snapping and barking at the great, but the things he said were so amusing, his manner so whimsical and homely that she was utterly absorbed. Then he asked about her fiancé, about his background and prospects, when they were going to be married and where they were going to live, and gave so much the impression of being concerned, not with anything in the past or future but simply with the relationship between the two of them, that she felt something inside her melting with pleasure. She was half-expecting all the time to find an intrusive hand placed upon her knee or arm, but Ocky did not so much as make a gesture towards her during a ride which she was afterwards to remember as one of the pleasantest half hours of her life.

When they arrived *The Plain Man* cameras were there, and so was a television newsreel van. A crowd of some seventy or eighty people cheered enthusiastically as the dumpy figure stepped out of the Rolls. The largesse that occasioned their presence had been distributed by Jimmy Crundle, but they rightly recognised Ocky as its source. The house was dingy, but it looked reasonably clean. Ocky stood on the steps of it with the newsreel interviewer.

"You were responsible for moving the Camerons out of their other flat, weren't you, Mr Gaye?"

"That's right. Jeannie Cameron appealed to me, and when I found out what their living conditions were like I was shocked, deeply shocked."

"But now they're moving back into the same district. Why is that?"

"We'd found them a nice little house but, quite frankly, they were lonely away from their neighbours. They wanted to be back here, and I'm delighted that *The Plain Man* was able to arrange it."

"Wasn't this an expensive business?"

"I want people to be happy. Hang the expense. I wish the Government thought the same way."

Ocky laughed and the interviewer dutifully laughed with him, then said, "But there's a lot of difference between a private organisation rehousing one family, and a Government subsidy which would involve thousands of families. Don't you think the cost would be prohibitive?"

A forefinger wagged. "And don't you think there's a lot of difference between the amount a private organisation can spend and the money the Government can afford? Don't bother to answer that one. But let me just tell you that the Cameron family are the spearhead of *The Plain Man*'s Housing Crusade. And here they are." He extended one arm. "The Camerons are coming."

They turned the corner now, in the van Jimmy Crundle had hired, Mrs Cameron and Jeannie, Rickie and the other children, Dad with his arms crossed, ready to criticise. But even Dad melted at sight of the cheering crowd and the television cameras. Mrs Cameron wept, Jeannie kissed Ocky. Rickie, still wearing his "Arab" jacket, exchanged friendly blows with other boys similarly jacketed. It was what might be called a reunion. Nobody could doubt that the Camerons were happy to be back. When Ocky left, the bits of furniture brought back from the despised suburb were being dragged upstairs, and Dad had gone off with half a dozen neighbours for drinks at the local.

When they left Jimmy came with them. He looked nervously at Ocky, said questioningly, "That wasn't so bad."

Ocky offered Jimmy a cigar, raised eyebrows at Mercury for permission, then lit one himself. "Don't be modest, Jimmy, it was very good indeed. Perfect. You're the man who said it couldn't be done. And you're the one who did it."

Jimmy smiled, then wiped his forehead.

Chapter Thirty-Three

The offices of the finance corporation – for it turned out to be that, not a firm of investment bankers – in which Masterson was a partner had about them a reassuring old-fashioned Victorian solidity. Outside there was a slightly decrepit commissionaire who wore a chestful of medals, inside the place had the unbustling male security of a London club. The lift creaked, and the lift-man pulled on a rope to take them up. Kirton sat for ten minutes in a waiting-room that offered a reading choice of *The Times* or the *Financial Times.* Then he was shown in.

Masterson sat behind a desk in a room with only one small window in it. They shook hands. Masterson said, "Well, Mr Kirton?"

He found it difficult to speak. "It's about Francie Lake."

"So I supposed."

"You know Deacon, Sir Daniel Deacon, committed suicide this morning. Ocky wanted him to put money into Plain Man Enterprises, a lot of money. Deacon wouldn't come in." Masterson stared at him across the desk. The expression on his face was heavy, brooding. "Ocky – Gaye – tried to force him. To blackmail him. I believe that's why Deacon committed suicide." With an effort he added, "I got the information that was used in the blackmail. I didn't know the way it was to be used, but I got it."

It was quiet in the room. A grandfather clock ticked in one corner. Masterson said, "Why do you bring this to me? If you carry your conscience round to anybody, it should be the police."

"I want you to show me that form of guarantee."

The bushy eyebrows knitted. "What an extraordinary suggestion."

"I believe it had something to do with Deacon's death. And I know Deacon's death was linked with Francie's murder. Listen to me." He told Masterson about his call on Pillin. When he had done Masterson spoke in a voice that was harsh with anger.

"I don't know what you're talking about."

He was disconcerted. "What do you mean?"

"You come here and tell me this story. I don't know how much of it is true, you offer no proof of anything you say. But suppose it is true, who had a motive for stealing those pictures? Deacon, nobody else."

"I've told you, the pictures were fakes."

"That's what this photographer said, but do you trust him? From what you've told me, you don't trust anybody. The way I read what you say, the way any sensible man would read it, is that Deacon knew about these pictures – and even if they were fakes, they'd have been enough to ruin him – and killed this woman to get them. Then he shot himself, when things got too difficult for him. If I accept what you tell me, that's the conclusion I would draw, but I don't see why I should accept it. You've made insinuations without a fragment of proof. Shall I tell you what I really think, Kirton? I believe this is a put-up job on your part, a deliberate blackening of Deacon's name by which you're trying to put the screw on Ocky Gaye."

"I've put it all badly." But looking at Masterson's face he sensed his defeat. "Deacon couldn't have known about the pictures. He fell into a trap."

186

"I've nothing more to say to you." Masterson pressed a button on his desk. Beside it, Kirton saw a photograph of Jennifer.

Desperately he said, "Tell me this. If Deacon wouldn't come in with Ocky, why should he sign the guarantee form?"

"I don't know what you're suggesting. His name was only one of six on the form. Another of the names is mine."

To the secretary who appeared in the doorway Masterson said, "Show this gentleman out."

Chapter Thirty-Four

Nevers looked at his watch, then said to Quick, "Time to go."

"Go where?"

"To see our TV show, of course." He tapped the sheets sent him by McClintock. "This gives us an idea of the approach they're making, but I want to talk to Gaye and this producer fellow before they go on the air to make quite sure they don't stray outside the limits. The purpose of this operation from our point of view is to put pressure on Stead. He's back at *The Plain Man* office, you say."

"That's right. Looks pretty white around the gills, I'm told."

"He'll look whiter by the time I've done with him. I think he should come along to see the show, don't you? I'll ring Gaye and tell him to make sure of it."

Nevers' telephone call did nothing to affect Ocky's good temper. He said to Mercury, "Bill's in his office, we'll take him along with us to the show, just tell him, will you. And I'd like to see him here in five minutes' time."

He returned to his exposition of the great Housing Crusade. The rehousing of the Camerons was only a beginning, there were Camerons all over the country, people who were longing to live in better conditions, to get away from extortionate landlords. Why should there not be a Plain Man Estate, a model for all such estates, no wretched restrictions like those in the suburb the Camerons had hated so much. Why should they not offer each week in the paper a home on this model estate for one family? His thoughts soared onwards and upwards. Dex and Jimmy listened, more or less spellbound, until Ocky broke off abruptly as Bill Stead entered the room.

"I ought to be getting down and having a word with Alex," Jimmy said. Dex, it appeared, had a date with Marian. Ocky waved them both away and concentrated the full warmth of his gaze upon a paper-pale Bill Stead.

"Now, Bill, I've called you in to say this. I don't want you to worry. What your troubles are with the police I don't exactly know, but – "

"I told them a few lies. But I've made another statement now, and it's the truth."

"What I do want you to know is that I'm right with you. I'm on your side. I said to Nevers, 'Bill's a good lad and I'll be delighted if you can tell me he's in the clear now,' and he said that he was satisfied. I'm not asking for details, Bill, but what I want to say especially is this. I want you to come along and watch tonight's show. I want you to look at the evidence we're going to present, and then afterwards to comment in any way you like on it. I believe you'll be able to clear yourself of any suspicions that may, I only say may, attach to you."

"All right."

Ocky put an arm round his shoulders. "You loved her, Bill, I know that. I loved her too. We miss her."

Rather pettishly Stead said, "I didn't love her. I dare say that was half the trouble."

Ocky removed the arm. "Anyway, you'll come with me. And with Boy Kirton. Where is Boy?" He called in Mercury, and learned that Kirton had not come back. A shade of annoyance passed across his brow and was gone. Mercury was more concerned, feeling that Kirton's absence was in some way a reflection on her efficiency.

"It's unlike Mr Kirton. He had a note of the time too. We really should be going."

"Then let's go. He'll be there."

Ocky sat in the back of the Rolls with Stead, silent and gloomy, on one side of him and Mercury on the other. On the way he told Stead all about the Cameron rehousing, making the whole thing into a joke but without losing sight of its serious, and indeed moral, implications. Mercury interrupted once to wonder what could have happened to Mr Kirton, and Ocky breezily repeated that they would probably find him waiting for them. But when they drew up outside Francie's flat he was not there.

Chapter Thirty-Five

Francie's flat, and the flat above it which had been commandeered for the evening at a handsome price, were in what seemed to be complete chaos. The sitting-room of the flat was a mass of trailing cables. Men were clambering up on ladders fixing lights, other men were shifting the sofa on which Ocky and Kirton were to talk in the winding-up scene that was to be shot in the flat, others still were marking the floor to show the points at which Ocky was to rise from the sofa and walk five paces backwards and forwards before making his peroration. The flat seemed to have been taken over completely by these technicians, so that any outsider hearing them in earnest consultation with McClintock would have thought that the human elements appearing in the show could have got into it only through an oversight. McClintock spared a worried smile for Ocky and his troupe, then effortlessly transformed this smile into a frown.

"Where's Boy? Don't tell me he's not with you, really it's too much. Jimmy, you're supposed to be looking after that."

"I thought he'd be here."

"He's not." McClintock stared accusingly from one to the other of them. "Do you mean to say that nobody knows where he is?"

Jimmy mumbled something unintelligible. Ocky raised a plump hand. "You mustn't blame Jimmy, he's been working on an urgent job for me. Boy went out this afternoon and he's not come back."

"Not come back!"

"Don't worry, Alex, he'll be here."

The tide of technicians swept over them both. If Ocky walked backwards and forwards, it seemed, he couldn't be lighted properly. Ocky obligingly came and sat where they told him, stood where they told him, strutted diagonally across the room instead of strutting parallel to a wall. Jimmy wiped his forehead.

"Mercury, my dear, you'd better go and ring Boy's flat, if that's no good try anywhere else you can think of."

"What's the point of ringing the flat? He won't be there now."

"Well, do something, girl, do something." He pushed her out of the room. "You've no idea where he might be, have you, Bill?"

Stead was standing just inside the door, with his hands in his jacket pockets. He did not answer. Jimmy, exasperated, repeated the question and was disconcerted to find it echoed behind him. He turned to find Superintendent Nevers and Sergeant Quick.

"Would it be Mr Kirton you're looking for?"

Jimmy's feeling in relation to the police was always one of guilt. He nodded.

"Then I can put your mind at rest," the superintendent said heartily. "Mr Kirton rang the office, but you'd left. He asked me to let you know that he's on his way. He'll be here in a few minutes."

McClintock was shouting. "There are too many bloody people in this room. We've got a programme to put out in half an hour and I want everybody who's not connected with it outside." His assistant, a young man with a blond crew-cut, began to shoo people towards the door, flapping his arms as though they were geese.

"I take it this means us, Quick," Nevers said cheerfully. "Unless, of course, you're ambitious to appear in the programme." Quick, who had been goggling across the room at

Ocky, started. Nevers put a hand on Jimmy's shoulder. Jimmy flinched away. "We'll make ourselves as obscure as possible, but I want a word with Mr Gaye before the programme starts."

At this moment Ocky, who had been taking steps across the floor as though he were playing a discreet version of hopscotch, saw Nevers and came towards him with hands outstretched, a wide smile on his face. His greeting somehow managed also to embrace Quick and Bill Stead.

"Delighted, just delighted to see you again, and the sergeant." Quick blushed. "But what have you been saying to young Bill here? You really had me worried, I don't like my boys getting into any kind of trouble. I was really glad to be able to tell Bill that you were satisfied with his last statement. That's right, isn't it, Bill?"

Stead bent upon them a white, agonised gaze. "If you want to know, I don't give a damn about what any of you think." Ocky and Nevers both looked at him. Behind them the assistant director was saying *Please, please.* "I don't know how you can come here and do this sort of thing when it's only a few days since she – " He did not complete the sentence, but turned and went out.

Ocky was prepared to be benevolent. "He's upset."

"You had no right to tell him I was satisfied," Nevers said sharply.

"I simply repeated your own words. You said to me, 'We're satisfied for the moment.' Those were your very words."

"For the moment."

"We all live by the moment, don't we? I know I do."

"Come along now, *please.* All upstairs. We've got a programme to put out."

They allowed themselves to be pushed out of the room and into the passageway outside the flat. Nevers, as they stood there, said to Ocky, "I must impress on you again, Mr Gaye, that there are very strict limits to what may be said in this programme. The general outline you gave me is to be adhered to absolutely."

Ocky was nodding his head. He did not appear to be listening and his answer was hardly relevant. "We'll do all we can to help you, rely on that."

"I shall want an assurance from Mr McClintock to the same effect. No names to be mentioned."

The producer pushed his way towards them. Ocky said, "I don't think you've met. Superintendent Nevers, our producer, Alex McClintock. And this is Sergeant Quick. The superintendent wants an assurance that we shan't depart from that general outline – "

"He needn't worry. We shan't have any bloody programme if that bastard Kirton doesn't show up. Doesn't anybody know – "

A taxi stopped outside the flat. Kirton stepped out of it.

Chapter Thirty-Six

They sat in the room upstairs, watching the images in the square box. Ocky was at one end of a semi-circular row of chairs, hands folded placidly in his lap. Mercury sat next to him, then came Stead and Jimmy Crundle, Nevers and Quick, and finally Kirton at the other end of the row. Ocky and Kirton had exchanged only a dozen words.

"You cut it fine, Boy."

"I was busy."

"I know," Ocky said amiably. "Ray Pillin told me."

They looked at each other. Then Ocky's face, benevolent but stern, appeared on the screen, and he was talking in a voice rich, warm and beautifully controlled.

"Tonight we are bringing you the most unusual programme you have ever seen on television. You are going to watch a first-hand investigation into a murder that occurred less than seventy-two hours ago. This was the victim." A photograph of Francie appeared on the screen. "Her name was Francie Lake, and she had been an associate of mine since I first started *The Plain Man*. But Francie was more than a business associate, she was a dear friend. On the day that she died I decided that my organisation would investigate her death and would pass over immediately any information we obtained to the police authorities. This programme shows you a little of what we have been doing, and I acknowledge gratefully the permission given by the authorities to show you this film. If any one among the millions of you who are watching finds a single thing in it that may lead to the identification of Francie's murderer, then this experiment will have been publicly justified. As for my private feelings – well, I shall owe you a debt I can never repay."

With an effort Nevers looked away from the hypnotically powerful image on the screen and at the watchers. Ocky sat with chin in chubby hand, staring at himself in fascination. Mercury was dabbing at her eyes with a small handkerchief. Jimmy Crundle was looking at Ocky. Quick had his mouth slightly open. Kirton's face was impassive, and remained so now that he appeared on the screen himself, talking to Smedley. A map appeared, showing Francie's movements on Tuesday evening, the drink in the *British Volunteer*, then her journey home in the taxi. Ocky was seen again, finger raised.

"She reached home at a quarter to eight, or a little after it, that evening. On the following morning she was found brutally stabbed to death. Some time that evening she was visited by her murderer. Who was it? Here are some of the clues – if they are clues – left in the flat. First of all, this letter, which was found in the typewriter – "

Alex McClintock appeared in the doorway, said, "Come on." Ocky and Kirton rose and followed him. They went into the room downstairs where the cameras were set up. "You know exactly what you're doing, right?" the producer said. "Three points for discussion, the letter, the *Criminal Guide*, the book. And no names, that's understood."

Ocky was almost amused. "We've done this sort of thing before." He pulled out his gold toothpick, pushed it about among his fine large teeth.

"Not with this sort of subject." McClintock ran a hand through his hair. Flecks of dandruff floated down. "Come on."

They took up the positions marked out for them, Ocky on the sofa in the living-room, Kirton beside the door. There was a television set down here on which they could see the last visits being made by the team of investigators. Outside in the street a car door shut, there were voices. Kirton jerked his head slightly. McClintock said angrily, "See who that is, and try to keep them quiet outside, will you."

The assistant producer went out. The interviews came to an end. McClintock raised his hand. Ocky began to speak.

Chapter Thirty-Seven

"I am now in Francie's flat. This is the living-room, in which her body was found, just over here." He got up and indicated the spot. "The book that she had pulled down was by her side. The letter I told you about was in the typewriter – over there. The catalogue that has been mentioned, the *Criminal Guide,* was in the bedroom just across there, beside the bed. Now I'm going to ask Mr Kirton – Boy Kirton, as we call him in the office – to say something about the conclusions we've reached from the investigation."

The camera's glare came on to Kirton. He felt as though he were participating, not in a play acted out upon a stage, but in some kind of dream sequence from a film. His weightless body was here, but his mind was surely not. He remembered exactly that first restaurant luncheon. "Plovers' eggs. Of course you want them, boy. Look how much they cost." He had eaten the plovers' eggs, but had he liked them? It was important, and seemed impossible, to remember. With an effort that was physically painful he dragged himself away from the scene and spoke the words allotted to him in this much more fictitious one.

"First of all the catalogue. I saw the man who publishes the *Criminal Guide* and established from him that copies are only sent to subscribers. There are less than three hundred of them. All the copies of this particular issue were posted on Monday night, and should have reached the subscribers on Tuesday morning."

"Was Francie a subscriber?"

"No."

"Then she must have borrowed her copy of it – or it was left here by her murderer. You gave this information to the police, Boy?"

"I did."

"And they don't know of any explanation for the presence of this catalogue in the flat? Nobody has come forward to say that they loaned her a copy?"

"I understand not."

"Very interesting." Ocky looked straight into the camera and held it, a significant pause. "Now the letter."

"Yes. I don't believe that this letter was typed by Francie Lake."

"Why not?"

"Francie was English. Certain phrases in the letter are distinctly American. 'Will you please accept this letter as my resignation, *as of now.*' Then later on, '*I want out.*' These aren't English phrases. A couple of lines later the word *grey* is spelt in the American manner – g-r-a-y. Later still, the word 'fender' is used instead of the English 'mudguard.'"

Ocky looked deeply impressed. "That sounds conclusive. It seems, then, that an American wrote this letter. Very important. What about the book?"

"The book contains the name of somebody involved in the case."

"Somebody Francie knew well?"

"Yes."

"And this person," Ocky spaced out the words, "is an American, and also a subscriber to the *Criminal Guide*?"

"Yes," Kirton said again. His mouth was dry.

Upstairs Bill Stead moaned and put his head in his hands. Jimmy Crundle moved away from him as though he were contaminated. Nevers also got up, walked out of the room and down the stairs. In the entrance hall a tall young girl was arguing with the producer.

"I'm very sorry, you'll just have to go out," McClintock said in a penetrating whisper. "There's no question of your appearing. The show's almost finished. Mr Gaye's winding it up now."

The girl whispered back at him. "Just let me stay here for five minutes. My name's Jennifer Masterson, and I've got – "

Nevers put a hand on McClintock's shoulder, swung him round. His voice was furious as he said, "Did you know Gaye was going to draw conclusions pointing to a particular person?"

"I thought as long as we avoided names – "

Nevers muttered something impolite, pushed him away.

Upstairs on the screen Ocky's face stared into the room, solemnly parsonical, his voice rich with clerical unction.

"So these are the vitally important results of an investigation which is still in progress. We have established that there are grounds for thinking that one of the persons who could, as the saying is, help the police in their investigations, is an American who knew Francie well, whose name appears in the book that she pulled down before she died, and who typed the letter which – "

"No."

The watchers in the passage could see the set inside the room. Kirton's face was not visible, but his voice expelled the monosyllable as though it came out of a hose in which a steam jet had been suddenly turned on. Jennifer Masterson gave a sigh of pleasure. McClintock stared at the set, appalled. The cameras switched agitatedly from Ocky, caught in mid-delivery, to Kirton staring at him across the room, back to Ocky and again to Kirton, who said deliberately, "This is a frame-up."

Now Kirton spoke much more quickly and jerkily, clearing his throat occasionally, twisting his fingers together. "The frame-up was arranged by the murderer. The American phrases in the letter were meant to be noticed, and if I'd not seen them they would soon have been spotted by somebody else. In fact the American in question, who works in our organisation, is so much Anglicised that he'd never say or write 'fender' for 'mudguard.' The book was planted by the murderer as a clue pointing to the American – Francie never took it down from the shelf. The *Criminal Guide* was taken by the murderer from the American's room and put in the flat. The whole thing was a plant, and a fairly clumsy one."

Ocky kept himself perfectly under control. His own voice, unlike Kirton's, remained smooth and untroubled. "That's a fascinating theory, Boy, and I wish we had time to discuss it, but – "

"I know who arranged the plant." Kirton's finger jabbed out as though he were a puppet, his face was twitching. "You."

Chapter Thirty-Eight

McClintock came to life. "Cut it, cut it," he screamed. "For God's sake, cut it. Have they all gone mad, what do they think they're saying?" One of the engineers pulled a switch. The picture vanished from eight million sets. The producer stormed into the living-room. "Do you know what you've done?" he said to Kirton. "You've landed yourself in the biggest mess of your life."

"It went out on the screen?"

"My God, it did. You must be crazy."

"That's good. I wanted to pin him so that he couldn't get away."

"I believe you're really off your head," McClintock began, and then felt himself gently pushed aside. Nevers was standing in his place, looking at Ocky.

"I'm sure Mr Gaye will want an explanation from Mr Kirton."

"Not here and now." Ocky got up. "I don't think that what McClintock said is so far off the mark, Superintendent. Boy here is suffering from intense nervous strain. He needs a long rest."

"But I should like Mr Kirton to explain what he means. Here and now." Nevers made a gesture at the camera crews who stood staring at them and said to McClintock, "Get them away. And there's no need for you to stay, either. Ask Sergeant Quick to come down here, will you. And to bring Stead with him."

Kirton seemed to come to life. "Miss Masterson – she's outside, isn't she?"

Ocky probed with his toothpick. "I don't see what you're hoping to do, Boy. Except wreck a television programme, that is."

Kirton ignored him. "Can Miss Masterson come in? She has some important evidence."

"All right." Nevers said to Quick, whose ingenuous face showed extreme curiosity, "You'll find her outside. Bring her in, too. Then shut the door."

When they had come in they all stood or sat facing Ocky, rather as though he were still the image on the screen rather than the tubby figure in his all-too-evident flesh who composedly confronted them. There was a silence.

Nevers looked at Kirton. "Well?"

"I'm trying to think of the best point to begin."

"It's a pity you've got no money, Boy," Ocky said pleasantly. "It's no use suing you. I don't know what my position is in relation to the television company, in view of the fact that it's my own programme. It's a nice point."

"Perhaps the best way to start is with the fact that Plain Man Enterprises is on the skids. It's losing money hand over fist and you've said yourself that the situation is desperate. You said to me that I wouldn't like to see you dragged through the bankruptcy courts, right?"

"No argument." Ocky grinned. "That would be a terrible sight. But I've been in tight spots before."

"Yes. And you had a way out, a solution – temporary, of course, like all your solutions. Get Deacon to come in as a backer. But Deacon wanted complete control, so that fell through at the last minute. Agreed?"

"Agreed, Boy, agreed."

With an effort Kirton looked away from the amused reproach in Ocky's gaze, and addressed himself to Nevers. "He then tried to force Deacon in by blackmail. He told me to go down to Wales and dig into Deacon's past. I did it, and came up with an incident about Deacon and a young girl. Deacon may have been innocent or guilty, but Ocky decided to use it."

"You did that." This was Stead, morally indignant.

"Yes. I didn't know the way he was going to use it, but I did it."

Ocky interposed before Nevers could ask a question. "Agreed, agreed. You got some information for me about Dan Deacon. It was a serious situation, and, you never know when information may be useful."

"This is the way he used it." Kirton still looked at Nevers, not at Ocky nor at Jennifer. "Somehow he got hold of a young girl, and a man to impersonate Deacon. They went along to a hotel named the Eugene and there Ray Pillin took pictures of them going into the hotel, the man looking like Deacon and dressed like him. Then he took more pictures of them inside, half naked. These were the pictures Pillin took to Francie Lake's flat."

Nevers said harshly, "You've got proof?"

"I saw Pillin this afternoon and got all this out of him, including the name of the hotel. Then I saw the hotel manager and he confirmed what had happened."

"Denied," Ocky said promptly. "Absolutely and totally denied. What Ray may have been up to I don't know, but it had nothing at all to do with me."

"That isn't what he said this afternoon."

"Ray rang me after you'd left him. He told me that you'd nearly strangled him. Naturally, he said whatever you wanted him to say. Have you identified this man and girl that you say were involved?"

"No."

Ocky shook his head sadly, opened his mouth and then seemed to decide that comment was unnecessary.

"The blackmail of Deacon was linked with your need to put Francie out of the way. You planned to murder her and remove the photographs. Then you would tell Deacon that the pictures had been in her possession but now they'd vanished. So your blackmail plot provided Deacon with an overwhelming motive for murder. Your offer to him would have gone something like this. Put money into Plain Man Enterprises – on your terms and not on his – and you would be able to keep Pillin quiet and would destroy the negatives of the pictures. Faced with this threat, Deacon committed suicide."

Ocky shook his head again and murmured, almost sadly, "Proof, Boy, proof. You haven't a shred of it."

Kirton turned again to Nevers. "You must remember that I've found out most of this only today. I spoke on the telephone to Deacon's widow. She said that he" – Kirton found it difficult to say either *Ocky* or *Gaye* – "came to see her husband on Wednesday. Afterwards Deacon said that he was a low-down, thieving crook, that he wanted to ruin them and that he was never to be let into the house again. I also spoke to Deacon's office. His secretary told me that Deacon had been using a private detective and she thought it was something to do with Mr Gaye. No doubt you'll be able to find him."

"None of this is evidence, Superintendent, as you know as well as I do." Ocky took out his toothpick again, played with it, and put it back.

"You mentioned something about Miss Lake," Nevers said. "Why should he want to kill her?"

"He regarded her as his property, tied to him for ever. Now she was trying to break away, even hoping to get married. She was under a misconception there, because Bill Stead didn't want to divorce his wife, but still she was proposing to break away. He couldn't allow that."

"Is that all?" Nevers did not bother to hide his scepticism.

"No. She was in possession of information that, if she cared to use it, would ruin him and send him to prison."

There was silence again. Ocky suddenly said, "Hot in here. Mind if we have a window open?" He crossed to the windows looking out on to the street, threw up one of them, stood

205

breathing draughts of air. Kirton felt something melting inside himself. He thought, *You can never go on with this.* But when Ocky turned and he saw the broad, bland, half-smiling figure coming back into the ring for the next round, he knew that he could. He faced the little man directly now, and spoke his name.

"She never would have done it, Ocky, she never would have sold you out. You never understood what people were like inside, did you, only how to use them."

Ocky spread out his hands, appealed to Nevers. "In a minute I shall have to ask for protection, you know that? I just don't know what he's talking about? What does he mean when he says Francie could ruin me?"

"Just leave that, I'll explain it in a moment. Miss Masterson here knows what I'm talking about." Jennifer said nothing, sat with her hands between her knees, holding a brown leather briefcase. "Francie Lake was a queer woman, Ocky, desperately attached to you and determined to get away from you at the same time. That joke of hers about being dead, petrified Lake she called it, was typical. There was another thing she said in the pub that last night, that beneath her scaly exterior beat a heart too sensitive ever to wield the executioner's axe. She would never have used the axe on you, Ocky, but you didn't know that. You wouldn't let her go. You killed her, and then you framed Bill Stead for it because Bill was her lover."

Quick had been making notes. Now he put down his pencil and said with the air of a man at the end of his patience, "I don't know what he's talking about."

"Neither do I, Kirton." Nevers' voice was sharp. "What axe?"

Kirton ignored them. "You came along at some time in the small hours of Tuesday night, after giving your wife a sleeping-pill – "

"How do you know?" That was Nevers again.

"I don't. That's the way it works out, the way it must have been. At that time of night you needed only to take reasonable precautions and go in through the back entrance and the chances were high against you being seen. You killed her, took away Pillin's pictures and left an elaborate trail of false clues leading to Bill Stead, the book presumably dragged down by Francie, the fake letter, the copy of the catalogue. They were clues that would mean very little or nothing at all to the police, but could be picked up by somebody inside our organisation. I was the one chosen to pick them up. I can't forgive you for that."

He waited but Ocky said nothing. He went on. "You made a fuss about a Plain Man investigation, and put me in charge of it. You knew it wouldn't be long before I picked up the trail that led to Bill Stead."

Stead advanced across the room towards Ocky, arms outstretched, mouthing unintelligible words. Nevers said something to Quick. The sergeant jumped up, pinioned Stead's arms behind him. Ocky remained unmoved.

"Don't listen to him, Bill, can't you tell when a man's inventing? I'm waiting to hear him say something he can prove."

"You've got no talent for detail. The clues you planted were all either absurdly literary, like the book on the floor with Bill's name in it, or the Americanisms Bill doesn't use which you put into the letter – "

Still calmly, but with blistering viciousness, Ocky spoke. "You always were a stupid half-smart little bastard, weren't you, Boy? All you ever wanted was somebody who'd exercise authority over you, do all the things you were afraid of doing yourself." He paused, said distinctly, "You like to let other people do the dirty work. When your wife was killed, she was driving the car. I suppose you were too lazy or too drunk to drive."

He knew then that the hope of compromise had always been in his mind, the hope that somehow he might be spared from pushing things through to the end, and that now this hope had gone. He said to Nevers, "This is the sort of blackmail he uses.

I was driving the car when my wife was killed. He bribed the other driver to say my wife was driving our car. After that I did what he told me. He's reminding me of it now, warning me."

Ocky laughed out loud. "What did I say? He needs a rest."

"You asked for proof," Kirton said. "Here it is. You remember those guarantees? Francie went to see Masterson about them."

The superintendent nodded. "Masterson told me. They were a credit cover for *The Plain Man,* in the form of a guarantee from a holding company. What about them?"

"The signatures of the backers were forged."

"Nonsense. Masterson told me himself that he was one of the guarantors."

"I'll spell it out for you. The guarantee form was first issued five years ago. It was renewed each year, with the same names on it. But in those five years Ocky's reputation has taken a steep slide. People who would have visited his house five years ago wouldn't be seen in company with him now. Everybody knows this, everybody knows that in those five years *The Plain Man* has changed from a semi-radical weekly into the sort of semi-pornographic, semi-blackmailing rag-bag it is now."

Quick started to say something. Nevers stopped him. "Go on."

"Borboring and Graveley Wilson refused to renew their guarantees three years ago. Wiley Morecombe withdrew two years ago. Ocky couldn't get anyone to replace them, so he forged their signatures."

Nevers turned to Ocky, who spread out his hands. "If this were true, don't you suppose they'd be here to say so?"

Kirton's voice was hoarse as he said, "Jennifer."

She unzipped the briefcase. "Charles asked me to find out about this and I did. Here are letters from Lord Borboring and Mr Morecombe which confirm in writing what Charles has said. Sir Graveley Wilson didn't want to put anything in writing without talking to his lawyer."

"Admirable caution," Ocky said. Nevers looked at him then turned again to Kirton.

"Ocky realised this couldn't go on for ever. One day there would be a credit squeeze, or Masterson himself might decide to withdraw and approach the other guarantors to tell them so. Also, he was getting more and more into the red. If he could sell the company to Deacon it would be possible to scrap the guarantee forms. That was the vital importance to him of the Deacon negotiations. Deacon was interested in buying, but saw no reason why he should go on being a guarantor. Probably he thought his withdrawal might put on a bit of extra pressure in relation to the deal. So when the guarantee renewal came up a few weeks ago, he withdrew. Ocky had to forge his signature as well. He was careless and left one of his practice attempts at forgery lying around. Francie found it and made a guess at what he was doing – I discovered a sheet of paper in her desk, with an attempt on it to copy Deacon's name. She went to Ocky and he sent her along to Masterson, spinning a tale about her worry over the financial position and asking Masterson to show her the guarantee form. For good measure Masterson told her he was a signatory himself.

"So far so good, but Ocky knew she wouldn't leave it there. Being the kind of woman she was, she'd worry away until she got the truth. The collapse of the Deacon negotiations was the last straw. After that, Francie was bound to ask herself why Deacon should go on guaranteeing the paper's continued existence when he'd been stopped from buying it. Suppose she approached Deacon direct? Then the balloon would really go up." He looked at Ocky. "The odd thing is that I don't believe she would ever have done that. She was sick of her life on the paper, but she loved you too much to ever sell you out like that. But she wanted her freedom, and to you that would have been almost as bad. Thinking back over the way she talked those last couple of days, that's the way it works out."

Ocky had taken out the gold toothpick again and was tapping on the chair arm with it. He said to Nevers, "Do you want me to comment?" Nevers did not answer.

"You can see now what a difficult spot he was in," Kirton went on. "I don't know the exact financial position of the paper, but it's obviously pretty bad. Supposing it became necessary to call on the guarantors? That was one thing that worried him, another was the fear of exposure through Francie, and a third was that he found the whole situation intolerable. Things that belonged to him were his property forever. He never let go."

Ocky chuckled. "You really do make me out to be an ogre." He probed with the toothpick.

"You can see now what a master stroke the death of Francie seemed to be. First of all it got rid of her. Next, it provided a ready-made murderer in Bill Stead, who'd had the impertinence to be going around with her. Third, and most important of all, it offered a wonderful handle for blackmailing Deacon. But it all came unstuck. You didn't understand Francie, Ocky, and you didn't understand Deacon. You judged him by yourself. If you'd been put into a spot like that you'd have given way and tried to get your revenge later on. Deacon wasn't that sort of man. He killed himself sooner than go in with you. You looked shocked when you heard about his suicide and I can believe you were. It meant that you were still on the spot."

Nevers said, "Is that all, Mr Kirton?"

"I suppose so. Isn't it enough? If you get hold of Pillin – "

Nevers interrupted him. "Mr Gaye. You said something about commenting."

"What is there to comment on?"

Heavily the superintendent said, "An accusation of forgery."

"Oh, that." Ocky played with the toothpick, adjusted it. "I suppose there's no use in denying that, is there?"

With the same portentous heaviness Nevers said, "Not if it's true, sir, no. It can easily be proved."

"There it is, then. All my life I've been hampered from carrying out what I wanted to do by lack of money. Just before the war, you know there was a series of books called '*If I Were Dictator.*' A lot of people said what they'd do if they were given power in this country. I've often thought that the important thing isn't power but money. After all, power *is* money, isn't that so? Give me a sensible sum of money, ten million a year say, and within a few years I'd have changed the face of Britain."

"And the other matters?"

"Other matters? That stuff about blackmail and so on? You don't take that seriously, surely. Running a little crime magazine for me has gone to Boy's head."

"Not only blackmail. Murder."

"Naturally, I deny that too. I didn't suppose you were taking that seriously. After all, what proof has he got? There isn't a shadow of it, you must admit that."

"Mr Kirton has said a good many things that need investigation."

Ocky probed into his mouth for a particularly difficult piece of food. He winced, withdrew the toothpick and looked at it with satisfaction.

"I dare say. It's a pity I shan't be here to assist you."

"Not here? I don't understand you."

Ocky wagged a forefinger. "Don't think I admit for an instant any of that nonsense Boy was talking. I forgive him, but I don't admit any of it. The business about the guarantors is different, though. It's enough to send me to prison, and I shouldn't care for that. We agreed, didn't we, Boy, that it was impossible to imagine old Ocky in the bankruptcy court. Much more unimaginable, isn't it, that he should spend years in prison." He smiled at Kirton. "This is something I've been prepared for for a long time. Like the Romans, you know, but not in a bath. This toothpick – "

He stopped talking suddenly and put a hand to his throat. Quick sprang forward and caught the tubby body as it fell forward in the chair. Ocky's face was puffed and he was breathing stertorously.

"Get a doctor, Quick," Nevers said. He picked up the toothpick and looked at it. "Release this catch and it works like a hypodermic. Can't smell anything, I wonder what it is."

The sergeant looked up. "He's gone, sir."

The eyes were closed. The face that looked up at them was peaceful, on the lips a contented smile.

Chapter Thirty-Nine

"But we don't know," Jennifer said. "I mean to say, we don't *know*, do we?"

"Know what?"

"We know he forged the guarantees, but not that he killed Francie Lake. He never admitted it."

"Of course we know," Kirton said impatiently. They sat in the long bar of a pub just off Baker Street, eating sandwiches and drinking lager.

"No, we don't. For instance – " She drank some lager and considered. "For instance, when Mr Gaye – "

"Ocky."

"Ocky, then. When Ocky was setting his trap, how could he know that Deacon wouldn't be in a conference or at some meeting at the time he was supposed to be in the hotel?"

"He'd have made sure of it somehow." She had bitten into a ham sandwich, but even with her mouth full tried to articulate some protesting phrase. He amplified. "Ocky had a dozen different hangers-on of one sort or another, people like me who were bound to him through blackmail or gratitude, or a bit of both. He probably tricked Deacon somehow into meeting one of them that evening."

"Is that the best you can do?"

"That's the best I can do."

"Then you said he gave his wife a sleeping-pill. I suppose that's just a probability too."

"It's the way it works out, the way it must have been."

"The man who impersonated Deacon and the girl, where did they come from? You didn't explain how he found them."

"At a guess I should say through Shivers Stewart. He's a crook we've got in tow at the moment, ghosting his life story."

"That's just a guess."

"Nevers will find out, I expect, if he pushes things that far. He may be content to write off the whole thing now that Ocky's dead."

"It seems to me he was taking an awful risk. Ocky, I mean."

He shook his head. "Not really. Nobody else knew more than a fraction of the truth, not enough to do him harm. I knew one little bit of it, the man and the girl at the hotel knew another, Shivers Stewart – if that's who it was – knew another fraction of it, and so did Ray Pillin. None of us knew anything like the whole thing. If that side of it had gone as he expected, Deacon would have backed the paper and nothing more would have been heard about what went on at the hotel."

"You really haven't found out much, have you? You're not much of a detective."

"Perhaps not."

"What will happen now? To *The Plain Man*, I mean."

"If it's as much in the red as he said it was, I suppose it will go into liquidation. Anyway, *The Plain Man* was Ocky. Now that he's dead it's dead too."

"That will be a good thing." She looked at him with innocent eyes and said ruthlessly, "I mean, he was never the sort of man you thought he was. He was just a crook all the time."

He felt as though he were betraying some essential part of himself as he said, "I suppose so."

"What are you going to do now?"

"I don't know. I'll tell you something Ocky said to me the second time we met. 'All work corrupts,' he said, 'And working for Ocky Gaye corrupts completely.' He was speaking the truth.

When something like this happens to you it's final, you never recover."

"Nonsense." She spoke with the assurance of youth. "That's just nonsense."

"It's what I feel now, anyway. As though I shall never recover."

"You will." She stretched out her hand to him across the table, the nails short and grubby, a schoolgirl's hand. "I could help you to try."

Julian Symons

The Broken Penny

An Eastern-bloc country, shaped like a broken penny, was being torn apart by warring resistance movements. Only one man could unite the hostile factions – Professor Jacob Arbitzer. Arbitzer, smuggled into the country by Charles Garden during the Second World War, has risen to become president, only to have to be smuggled out again when the communists gained control. Under pressure from the British Government who want him reinstated, Arbitzer agreed to return on one condition – that Charles Garden again escort him. *The Broken Penny* is a thrilling spy adventure brilliantly recreating the chilling conditions of the Cold War.

'Thrills, horrors, tears and irony' – *Times Literary Supplement*

'The most exciting, astonishing and believable spy thriller to appear in years' – *The New York Times*

Julian Symons

The Colour of Murder

John Wilkins was a gentle, mild-mannered man who lived a simple, predictable life. So when he met a beautiful, irresistible girl his world was turned upside down. Looking at his wife, and thinking of the girl, everything turned red before his eyes – the colour of murder. Later, his mind a blank, his only defence was that he loved his wife far too much to hurt her...

'A book to delight every puzzle-suspense enthusiast'
– *The New York Times*

The End of Solomon Grundy

When a girl turns up dead in a Mayfair Mews, the police want to write it off as just another murdered prostitute, but Superintendent Manners isn't quite so sure. He is convinced that the key to the crime lies in The Dell – an affluent suburban housing estate. And in The Dell lives Solomon Grundy. Could he have killed the girl? So Superintendent Manners thinks.

Julian Symons

A Man Called Jones

The office party was in full swing so no one heard the shot – fired at close range through the back of Lionel Hargreaves, elder son of the founder of Hargreaves Advertising Agency. The killer left only one clue – a pair of yellow gloves – but it looked almost as if he had wanted them to be found. As Inspector Bland sets out to solve the murder, he encounters a deadly trail of deception, suspense – and two more dead bodies.

The Players and the Game

'Count Dracula meets Bonnie Parker. What will they do together? The vampire you'd hate to love, sinister and debonair, sinks those eye teeth into Bonnie's succulent throat.'

Is this the beginning of a sadistic relationship or simply an extract from a psychopath's diary? Either way it marks the beginning of a dangerous game that is destined to end in chilling terror and bloody murder.

'Unusual, ingenious and fascinating as a poisonous snake'
– *Sunday Telegraph*

Julian Symons

The Plot Against Roger Rider

Roger Rider and Geoffrey Paradine had known each other since childhood. Roger was the intelligent, good-looking, successful one and Geoffrey was the one everyone else picked on. When years of suppressed anger, jealousy and frustration finally surfaced, Geoffrey took his revenge by sleeping with Roger's beautiful wife. Was this price enough for all those miserable years of putdowns? When Roger turned up dead the police certainly didn't think so.

'[Symons] is in diabolical top form' – *Washington Post*

OTHER TITLES BY JULIAN SYMONS AVAILABLE DIRECT
FROM HOUSE OF STRATUS

ALL HOUSE OF STRATUS BOOKS ARE AVAILABLE FROM GOOD BOOKSHOPS
OR DIRECT FROM THE PUBLISHER:

Internet: **www.houseofstratus.com** including author interviews, reviews, features.

Email: **sales@houseofstratus.com** please quote author, title and credit card details.

OTHER TITLES BY JULIAN SYMONS AVAILABLE DIRECT
FROM HOUSE OF STRATUS

Quantity	£	$(US)	$(CAN)	€
☐ THE PLAYERS AND THE GAME	6.99	11.50	15.99	11.50
☐ THE PLOT AGAINST ROGER RIDER	6.99	11.50	15.99	11.50
☐ THE PROGRESS OF A CRIME	6.99	11.50	15.99	11.50
☐ A THREE-PIPE PROBLEM	6.99	11.50	15.99	11.50
HISTORY/CRITICISM				
☐ BULLER'S CAMPAIGN	8.99	14.99	22.50	15.00
☐ THE TELL-TALE HEART: THE LIFE AND WORKS OF EDGAR ALLEN POE	8.99	14.99	22.50	15.00
☐ ENGLAND'S PRIDE	8.99	14.99	22.50	15.00
☐ THE GENERAL STRIKE	8.99	14.99	22.50	15.00
☐ HORATIO BOTTOMLEY	8.99	14.99	22.50	15.00
☐ THE THIRTIES	8.99	14.99	22.50	15.00
☐ THOMAS CARLYLE	8.99	14.99	22.50	15.00

ALL HOUSE OF STRATUS BOOKS ARE AVAILABLE FROM GOOD BOOKSHOPS
OR DIRECT FROM THE PUBLISHER:

Hotline: UK ONLY: 0800 169 1780, please quote author, title and credit card details.
INTERNATIONAL: +44 (0) 20 7494 6400, please quote author, title, and credit card details.

Send to: House of Stratus Sales Department
24c Old Burlington Street
London
W1X 1RL
UK

Please allow for postage costs charged per order plus an amount per book as set out in the tables below:

	£(Sterling)	$(US)	$(CAN)	€(Euros)
Cost per order				
UK	1.50	2.25	3.50	2.50
Europe	3.00	4.50	6.75	5.00
North America	3.00	4.50	6.75	5.00
Rest of World	3.00	4.50	6.75	5.00
Additional cost per book				
UK	0.50	0.75	1.15	0.85
Europe	1.00	1.50	2.30	1.70
North America	2.00	3.00	4.60	3.40
Rest of World	2.50	3.75	5.75	4.25

PLEASE SEND CHEQUE, POSTAL ORDER (STERLING ONLY), EUROCHEQUE, OR INTERNATIONAL MONEY ORDER (PLEASE CIRCLE METHOD OF PAYMENT YOU WISH TO USE)
MAKE PAYABLE TO: STRATUS HOLDINGS plc

Cost of book(s): ———— Example: 3 x books at £6.99 each: £20.97

Cost of order: ———— Example: £2.00 (Delivery to UK address)

Additional cost per book: ———— Example: 3 x £0.50: £1.50

Order total including postage: ———— Example: £24.47

Please tick currency you wish to use and add total amount of order:

☐ £ (Sterling) ☐ $ (US) ☐ $ (CAN) ☐ € (EUROS)

VISA, MASTERCARD, SWITCH, AMEX, SOLO, JCB:

☐ ☐ ☐ ☐ ☐ ☐ ☐ ☐ ☐ ☐ ☐ ☐ ☐ ☐ ☐ ☐ ☐ ☐ ☐

Issue number (Switch only):

☐ ☐ ☐

Start Date: **Expiry Date:**

☐☐ / ☐☐   ☐☐ / ☐☐

Signature: _____

NAME: _____

ADDRESS: _____

_____

POSTCODE: _____

Please allow 28 days for delivery.

Prices subject to change without notice.
Please tick box if you do not wish to receive any additional information. ☐

House of Stratus publishes many other titles in this genre; please check our website (**www.houseofstratus.com**) for more details.